ECHOES *OF*
MERCY

Ifeoma Irene Ugboma

ECHOES*OF*
MERCY

Ifeoma Irene Ugboma

National Library of Nigeria Cataloguing-in-
Publication Data

Cover Design: Akila Jibrin

Printed and Published in Nigeria by:
Words Rhymes & Rhythm Limited
Suite C309, Global Plaza Plot 366, Obafemi
Awolowo Way, Jabi District, Abuja, Nigeria.
08169027757, 08060109295
www.wrr.ng

DEDICATION

To all those going through difficult moments, it is not yet over until you win.

To all the individuals who have wished of seeing God do wonders in their lives, He is still God and he is coming to you.

To the world, to prison inmates, to those who feel their sin is not pardonable, there is hope in Christ.

To my family, colleagues, Kismet foundation team, this book is for us all.

FOREWORD

Echoes of Mercy is a fiction that portrays how God works some times; how His ways are not our ways and how He shows mercy to whom He will show mercy.

No height is attained without people who continue to push you even across your limits;

To my beloved parents, thank you for your support, love and prayers.

To Obinwa Iheke Chima, you are a blessing and it was the inspiration you gave me that prompted this work.

Dr Victor Unung Abraham, thank you for supporting me all through.

To my talented editor, Buchi Onyegbule, thank you for honoring me with your literary art gift.

To friends, colleagues and acquaintances, thank you all for your unwavering support.

I love you all.

CHAPTER ONE

***when God starts with you, you become a surefire ***

It was a bright new day, and as early as the morning was, the sun shone with surprising intensity.

Daniel and his wife, Nancy were at home when George, their neighbor came knocking on their door. Nancy opened the door, a smile dancing at the corners of her mouth. Her eyes met George's.

"Good morning, George. How are you? Please come in." She said, offering him a seat in their meticulously arranged living room. "I hope all is well?" she added.

George gave her a wry smile as he sat down on their leather sofa; he had tried relentlessly to invite the Daniels over for a revival meeting all to no avail. Judging from his persistence, it was easy to surmise that he was bent on converting them to fervent Christians. The Daniels being a welcoming couple, had never refused opening their doors to him whenever he knocked, despite adamantly refusing to give in.

"Yes, Nancy. All is well. I just came to invite you and Daniel to a revival meeting in our church tomorrow. I pray both of you will be free to come around this time that is why I am inviting you guys ahead of time." He replied Nancy who returned a knowing smile. It had become a norm, George inviting them and them turning him down. Nancy hummed, "Okay George, we've heard you. We will have to think about it this time around okay?"

George smiled again knowing what the reply would be the following morning. He glanced at Daniel who did and said nothing. The thought of someone inviting him over for a revival meeting did not tickle Daniel's fancy.

He decided to keep mute rather than annoy his neighbor with unkind thoughts. "Poor George," he thought to himself, "wasting his life in these revival meetings he always attended."

He smiled to himself upon recalling how useless his life would have been if he was still meddling with shackles of Christianity. "What a waste", he said to himself.

"Honey, George is saying hello," Nancy said, interrupting his thoughts.

"George, you should know that my wife and I are not religious people and it will be an honor if you would respect our decision and stop inviting us to religious meetings, thank you." He blurted. On realizing how awkward he sounded, he searched for words to make his words seem less awkward, but couldn't find any.

"Okay George, will you have some tea?" Nancy asked, attempting to divert attention from her husband's outburst.

"No dear, I should be on my way now. Thank you so much for your time." He rose to leave, and Nancy walked him to the door. She turned to Daniel who seemed to have a strange smile hovering around the corner of his lips. He let out a mocking laughter and motioned his wife to come closer to him. Nancy drew closer and took a look at her husband. He was the only man that she had known since her parents died in an auto crash. She had known him for twelve years and had been married to him for six years. Their home have been filled with so much peace and understanding. Indeed, the fate that intertwined them was a strong one. They had gone through trials and tribulation, but still waxed strong despite moments when people turned their backs on them. She smiled, her eyes still fixed on him.

Christianity, this belief that seemed to annoy but yet amuse Daniel; she herself wasn't really religious, but she wondered what was so important about the faith that George kept trying to persuade them to come for their revival meetings.

Her knowledge of Christianity was rudimentary at best - Jesus died to save sins of the world. 'Is there any other thing special about this gathering of theirs anyway?' she wondered.

"Dannie, can't we just try this religious meeting out someday? It can turn out to be insightful you know?" She asked her husband, wrapped in his arms.

She immediately felt his arm lose its grip

"No Nancy, no!" He bellowed.

"I grew up with those religious people and believe me when I say it is no fun at all, the atmosphere is usually gloomy at those meetings and I have sworn that now that I am a man, I will never be part of such ever again!"

She smiled. Of course she expected that answer from him, but what amused her was how she had completely bought Daniel's idea of gloomy Christianity even without knowing much about it.

Something in her seemed to want to know more. George seemed so happy and at peace talking about this God who gave people second chances. George had obviously known God all his life and he didn't seem to be regretting it.

There had to be better things to do every day other than her usual routine of sleeping, waking and enjoying her husband's money. It might not be a bad idea anyway.

Usually, she would unhesitatingly have agreed with her husband, but right now she wanted to know what had kept George going with this faith of his. She wasn't sure yet about partaking in their meetings but she wanted to know how George had been enjoying his life with this faith Daniel despised.

"I am not saying we should be part of their Christian faith, but let's just attend to fulfill all righteousness and maybe George will leave us alone."

She said these without recognizing how high pitched her voice sounded.

Daniel stared in bewilderment and confusion. "What had gotten into her just now?" He wondered. He knew he didn't want to talk about the meeting neither did he want to argue with his wife.

"Darling you can go if you wish to, but for me, religion is out! End of this topic please."

Daniel rose and walked down the hallway while Nancy's gaze fixed on him as he walked. This was the part where she'd follow him to the bedroom and make up for the bad mood George tried to put them in, but here she was, still fixed on the couch, staring into empty space and hoping that Daniel would turn back and say yes to her request.

This her adamant Daniel, her anti-Christian husband with the golden heart. She erased thoughts of his reluctance from her mind and decided to go anyway, whether or not he went with her. She'd probably use it as her own research on Christianity and gauge her reactions to the belief.

Gathering resolve, she said, not sure if she was loud enough for Daniel to hear.

"I am going with George tomorrow; there is no harm in trying anyways." She said and rose to leave.

CHAPTER TWO

God has always been there, He never left

It was a misty Saturday morning, the forecast predicted rain any time soon, but judging from how busy the street was, individuals living in the suburbs were not overly worried.

Saturdays were usually laid back days for Daniel and Nancy as they were used to spending time together, attending parties or visiting friends.

Years had gone by in their marriage and they never made it a priority to have a baby, Nancy because wouldn't have her adorable physique ruined with pregnancy fat and Daniel didn't consider babies a necessity on his side. This however paved a way for the series of vacuum aspirations she had undergone.

A smile danced around the corners of her mouth as Nancy dressed herself up, adorned with jewelries, a chiffon dress and a pair of stilettos, she smiled to herself as she watched her husband grope past the morning newspaper for his cup of coffee.

When he noticed her standing, he smiled, his gaze fixed on her alluring physique adorned in her lovely apparel. He blessed the day fate honored him with his wife. Although lost in thoughts of his beautiful wife, something brought him out of it. "Wait, you are really serious about this church stuff? Because you looked ridiculous even talking about it", he found himself laughing again.

"I had to get your attention somehow Dan." She finally said as she turned her back to see Daniel staring at her wide-eyed.

"How do you mean?" He asked, his eyes alight in the hope of a midday nookie.

"I mean, let's go to this religious meeting George has been talking about...It can be a nice gathering, honey." Nancy pleaded.

Daniel abruptly laid aside the newspaper he was holding, the surge of hope that rose in him instantly faded away, and in place of it, was a disbelief he couldn't hide.

"You are that free Nancy? Don't you have anything to do with your life today?" He asked, slightly irritated. "You know this has never been part of our lives. What do you intend on doing there? It's a religious meeting and religion is out..."

He stopped at the appeal in her eyes. He had never denied her any single request, how was he going to stand by his words without hurting her?

"Why, Nancy? If you are curious about visiting the church then go ahead, besides the church will be happy to have you as member, even George will be glad if you go with him but count me out. "

He stood up and walked away, oblivious of her gaze on him. She checked her wrist-watch and gasped, she was late for her grocery shopping.

Nancy hummed as she dressed. A great sense of expectancy had stayed with her throughout the morning as she adjusted her beret to a saucy style; she turned toward the living room where Dan sat reading the sports page. He raised his eyebrows and let out the mocking laughter that could made her doubts resurface, just for a bit though, as she leaned into him in response.

"Just where do you think you are going my love?" He asked.

Nancy entwined her hands to his, pulling him to his feet, laying her head on his shoulder.

"I'm going with George, don't you remember?" Dan looked at her surprisingly; the unpleasant memories of his past life and how he hated religion rose in his mind. He wanted to say no to her but looking at her, he knew she wouldn't take that for an answer.

"I haven't given it another thought. Do you mean you really want to go?"

With an unexpected earnestness she answered,

"Very much darling, won't you come with me?"

For a long, hopeful moment, his eyes searched her face. He wasn't going to go, but he knew it would be disheartening if he didn't oblige her the permission to attend.

"If you really want to go, it's okay with me. You can tell me about it when you get home and we'll have a good laugh together." Nancy smiled, not surprised at her husband's unwavering stand on religion.

At this juncture, her curiosity had won her over. She wanted to find out what it was about this religion that Daniel had come to detest and George loved with everything in him. She gave him a peck and rushed out of the house knowing that Daniel was likely to change his mind within seconds.

Daniel lay on their bed, the rain that had threatened earlier now pattered gently on the roof of their house. He couldn't sleep, lying wide-eyed, looking on the ceiling as if there was an inscription there for him to read.

He was waiting for his wife and wondering what might have been keeping her this late. He slept off quite uneasily. The increasing sound of the rain invaded his dreams and his heavy body twitched to some unknown discord. There was a noisy mingling of faces, shapes and waters in his dream. There was a voice calling him, it became louder and the tempo got him up from his sleep, half an hour sleep.

His eyes fluttered open. "What was that?" He asked in confusion and jumped out of the bed on realizing that his wife was still not back.

At church, Nancy was seated at the front row on a plastic chair. The noise around her was ugly. At first, she couldn't deal with the chaos there; people laughing boisterously and greeting each other with hugs. She motioned frantically at George. She had assumed her visit here was going to be interesting and not just a raucous babble of pleasantries and other unending niceties. Obviously she had wrong expectations.

Suddenly there were frantic screams coming from a group on the other side, a woman was kneeling in their midst and the rest encircled her. "What are they doing there?" She wondered to herself, this must be the weird part Daniel talked about.

"They are praying for her, Nancy." George who seemed to have read her mind told her with a smile on his lips. Nancy returned the smile with so much effort, she was already disappointed. Her questions were cut short when a man walked up to the altar, one could tell he was the person in charge, the pastor. She exchanged glances with George who smiled in return. She was ready for the next drama that would happen, waiting to see if anything would captivate her because so far, none had.

The clergyman stepped onto the podium. He addressed the congregation humbly, taking verses from the Bible and explaining them so that everyone could understand.

Nancy found herself flowing in the welcoming atmosphere of the church now, as the pastor was speaking with a lot of authority proffered from the bible. She found herself captivated and gripped in an unusual way by every word that the preacher uttered. She even caught herself shedding a few tears at how overwhelmed she was at the word of God. What is this that was overtaking her being so? This pastor is good at this, she thought to herself.

"...While we were yet sinners Christ died for us. That is what the scripture says. In God we have life and an abundant life is certain in him. Our God loves us so much that he sent his only begotten son, Jesus to come die for us on the cross of Calvary. The love of God is so profound that it actually transcends human understanding. The willingness of God to give his only son to suffer and die for the world so that an access or passage-way can be made through which we can commune with him shows how much he wants a relationship with us...Are you pressurized by the outside world? Have you been living in sin? Are you backsliding in faith? God is ever willing to welcome you home, just open your heart for him. Praise the Lord!"

Something in her heart clicked. "This is for me," she said to herself, subconsciously. "This is for me."

"Brethren, if you are here and God is ministering unto you to surrender your life to him I want you to take a step of faith and march forward to this rostrum. God is willing to change you, he is willing to cleanse you and make you whole... Please step forward," The man of God urged, convinced that God had spoken to some people.

Something was pulling her to stand up and walk towards the altar but she couldn't let herself get up. She had better fight the urge to get up. What if walking out and confessing how reckless and carefree she has been living changes her life and marriage? Was this what Daniel dreaded? How come she believed so much about this God whom she barely knew, just like that?

She inexplicably found herself rising and walking down to the rostrum along with many others who wanted to surrender to God and let Him take charge of their lives. She reached the altar, knelt down as the pastor laid his hands upon each of them and prayed for them, and then one of the assistants led them into a separate room for counseling.

When the service was over, Nancy walked out of the auditorium feeling relieved and amazed at how simple it was to have gotten over a sinful life in split seconds with a minute-long prayer. She promised herself to learn how to pray each day, how to adapt to the new lifestyle she was going to embrace. She was grateful to God for forgiving her and to George for bringing her here. Indeed, her life seemed to have taken a new turn.

Daniel heard a knock at the door and quickly went to check who it was, hoping it would be Nancy but was disappointed to see it was the postman. The postman handed him an invitation card, then left after Daniel signed and thanked him. He opened the invitation card. It was an invitation from Edward for a cocktail party at his place by the end of the month. He glanced at his wrist-watch, then went back inside and closed the door.

The next few hours passed very slowly for Daniel, he repeatedly glanced at his watch, his patience wearing thinner with each glance. Finally, his anger and impatience took the best of him, so he aggressively hurled the book he had been reading to the wall opposite him.

"Is Nancy never coming back?" He wondered in frustration, hands akimbo.

A series of unwanted pictures rose unbidden in his mind. He saw the dull faces of the uncle and aunt who brought him up during his childhood. He thought of the ugly kitchen behind the store and the unappetizing food ladled ungraciously in his plate with a sharp admonition to be grateful there were good Christians willing to feed the likes of him. He also remembered the sadistic pleasures his uncle took in thrashing him if he failed to learn the scriptures assigned to him as his own portion of the reading, or if he wriggled during the long dry church services.

His uncle and aunt had been really religious people and the thought of them made him angry. He wondered what Nancy would be doing at a religious meeting; she was too intelligent to accept the kind of babble he associated with those gatherings.

He continued with his frantic glancing at his wrist-watch as he walked back and forth across the living-room, dropping into a chair and instantly rising again at the sound of light footsteps at the door. Finally, the door opened and Nancy walked in, her excitement tangible enough that he imagined he could taste it if he put out a tongue to it.

"Where have you been, honey?" He asked his wife apprehensively, almost letting out a tear in fear about the reason for her bubbly excitement.

She threw her arms around him and exclaimed, "Darling, I've found Christ!"

Daniel stood wide-eyed; he tried to calm himself down, the tension from waiting all evening for her having affected him so much. He tried to assimilate what Nancy had said. One of his greatest fears was to live that life again for the second time especially with someone he loves. He hugged her tight, letting go of the thoughts that invaded his mind. He had missed her a lot, and although he didn't fully understand what Nancy was saying, one thing was sure, he was not going to let her visit the church again.

"I am sorry for coming home late Dannie," She said.

The exasperation that had filled Daniel's soul left him, the hug was what he needed, it assured him that Nancy was still his and belongs to him, not any Christ or God.

CHAPTER THREE

smile, because you deserve to be happy

The week following Nancy's conversion was turbulent; Dan's reaction had been violent as though the very force of his anger would destroy her new faith. His wrath was only further incited by her gentle attempts to reason with him. He wasn't having it, he grew up with hatred for that God who seemed so carefree, who seemed apathetic when bad things happened to good people like his parents.

He was still a kid when they died in an auto crash, even though death is inevitable, must both of his parents die? That question haunted him till he became a man. He knew his parents to be religious people, practicing Christians, but when they needed God to save them from the claws of death, he abandoned them, leaving them to die on that miserable road and rendering him lone in this cold world, deserting him to the mercy of his mean uncle and aunt. Hell no! That religion had done him no good and he was not having it with his wife; he constantly reminded himself.

The cold November air greeted Nancy as she stepped out from the house, she had her flurry designer black shoes on and her cream and green colored dress. It was a Friday and she intended to visit the church for a fellowship. She was halted by Dan's rather harshly voiced question;

"And where on earth do you think you are going Nancy?"

Her heart sank, she wasn't prepared to have this argument with him again.

"Our new minister is preaching today, Daniel. Hope you don't mind me going honey?"

"Oh, you mean your new found love?" He asked sarcastically. He continued ignoring the appeal in her eye, insisting.

"I mind! For crying out loud Nancy what the hell do you think you are doing to yourself? To us? To our marriage? "

"Honey I am giving it a brighter life and the right way of living. I am sorry if the thought of religion is totally absurd to you but Dannie..."

At this point she took a deep breath, gauging her words carefully. "What I am doing is life! And I want you... "

Daniel cut her off immediately on realizing what she wanted to say. "You want me to follow you on your path towards misery huh? Bad news! I won't, not in this life!"

He turned his back to her and picked up a magazine lying on the table.

Nancy glanced at her watch, knowing that she'll be late if she didn't leave immediately. Her new found love for God at the moment had made her conscious of every little detail.

"I am sorry Dan, I am running late so I have to leave now," she said, fluttering her eyelashes innocently. Daniel laughed and she couldn't help but join in, oblivious of the reason he was laughing.

"Don't contaminate my home with your damned Christianity Nancy, I won't have it". He said with a more crazed voice than usual. She felt her face turn red, she wanted to cry. She opened her mouth to speak but found no words. Daniel stared at her with sympathy, but before her were two options: to walk into her car and drive away or to do her husband's bidding. Within her, she wanted to go but the thought of hurting Daniel by leaving made her hesitate.

Nancy's feet stuck to the ground, Daniel gazed at her, hoping she wouldn't dare defy him.

Daniel stood in awe as he watched his wife drive out of the compound without saying a word to him again. That was quite brave of his wife - this is what the "God thing" did to people, he thought; turn them to psychos.

He reminded himself again that he was in charge, not God or his Jesus.

Evenings that were normally filled with happy conversations is, today, shrouded with Dan's grim silence. Nancy tried to get her husband attention to no avail as Dan buried himself in some work he brought home. Nancy's fingers moved tightly over a bit of sewing. Now and then, she would look hopefully toward her husband, longing to talk with him and spy the little smile at the corner of his mouth.

Dan laid aside the paper on which he was working on and leaned back wearily. His eyes meet hers, and for a moment, he revealed a smile. He reached for his cigarette and offered a pack to her. Automatically, she reached for it then she withdrew her hand quickly.

Anger blazed in his eyes as he hurled words at her. "You have started again, haven't you?"

Her shocked face cut him to the bone but he couldn't stem the angry words that fell out of him in spurts.

"First, you now have this habit of praying every now and then, then giving up smoking, soon it will be something else. You will keep giving things up until there is nothing else – until your life is barren and empty. But you are not going to do it Nancy. I waited and dreamed, and worked too long to build our lives to have you destroy it now!"

Nancy caught his hand and knelt beside him. She really didn't know what to say, she had envisaged a strong reaction from him, but hadn't thought that the argument would linger on for days. Her eyes clouded with tears.

"Dan, Daniel what are you talking about, what had happened to make you feel you feel this way?"

He withdrew his hand from hers, his face showing his disappointment.

"You'd better give up your marriage or your religion!"

This broke her. The one man she had spent her whole life leaning on for joy and support was now giving her an ultimatum.

"How could you ask me to give up my marriage or Faith? Dan I love my marriage as much as I have come to love Christ. All you need to do is to find him also, give your life to Christ honey… surrender unto the light of His glory…."

The more she talked, the more his hatred for God grew. "Enough of this Nancy!" He growled.

"I will not let you ruin my home with your new madness; I curse the day I let you go to that revival meeting with George."

Daniel left the room with hopes that he had driven his point home. Whatever his wife was trying to achieve with this was a mystery he could not fathom. Was she trying to spite him? He was not going to let this escalate.

Nancy gave in to tears; she wailed. She didn't want to give up this new found faith but her husband was her life.

Weeks rolled by silently and quickly. And things went smoothly for the couple. For the first time in a couple of months, Nancy rekindled the bliss that had characterized their home by putting a stop to things that were deemed ugly, and worshiping and praying when her husband went out.

It was a Friday afternoon and the sun was out. Dan whistled as he inserted the key in the lock and swung open the door of his car. For a moment, the compliments they exchanged between themselves were forgotten as Nancy stepped out from the kitchen to where he stood. Her eyes brightened at the sight of him. He kissed her eagerly, then stepped back as he noticed her crisp, cotton dress.

"You'd better hurry honey... did you forget the party we were invited to by my friend?" Dan asked, slightly furrowing his brows.

"Oh Dan... "

For a moment she hesitated, and then her voice steadied. "I can't go with you Dan."

Dan dropped her hands, anger rising in him

"Yes, you are going with me Nancy. This religion thing has gone far enough."

He gripped her arm firmly, steering and dragging her towards the bedroom. Nancy stood wide-eyed as he threw open the closed door, his back still towards her. He pulled open a drawer and began roughly gathering up garments. As he turned, his stormy eyes met her quiet ones. Dropping the garments on the bed, he gripped her.

"You are going with me Nancy. Furthermore, you are going to take alcohol and whatever is offered to you. You are not going to snub our friends and you are not going to poison our home with religion. Now get dressed!"

Quietly, she answered, "I'm not going."

He shook her, his anger growing into a blind rage, lashing at her with all the venom of his hatred for religion.

"It's your religion or me Nancy. I won't come home to a house ruled by it."

Tears streamed down her cheeks as she answered. "You know how much I love you darling, but I can't dishonor my Lord by taking part in an affair like that again."

Blindly, Dan turned towards the living room. Nancy cried out, her worst nightmare was coming true.

"Darling, don't go! Oh Dan…"

He stopped, hope surging in him. "Don't you see I am not a religious man? Why can you not accept that?"

"No Dan, it's a religion I want you to accept. I want you to know Him dearest as your own savior and Lord."

For a moment he looked at her, torn between the thought of his hatred for God and his love for her. Then he turned and slammed the door. Tearfully, she called out to him but he didn't turn back. He drove away.

Her home seemed at the verge of wrecking, but she was not going to give up. This was her Daniel, she intended to break him; he needed to know that God was more than that weird picture he painted of him.

She planned to make Daniel a living miracle, but how was she going to do that when he was not willing to change? This was a harsh reality; she was certain she did not want to live a life of grief. She had toiled with Daniel, lived with him through hard times and swore to stand by him no matter what. Now that their life seemed to be getting easier, she was backing away from him because of her love for God. How can she live like this with Daniel? One night seemed to bring back hope, another, chaos. She was now faced with choices that she previously didn't know existed. She was confused on how to approach the current situation and afraid of what the future held but within her, she strongly believed his path was inclined with God's.

It had become her sole responsibility to make that happen no matter how hard it seemed. This had become her fight, and she was sure the God who had seen the present situation and had brought her thus far will see her through it all.

"I am not losing you Daniel, I cannot."

She said this to herself amid pain, fears, hope, expectations.

"This is going to hurt people I care about, but between harsh realities and living forever in paradise, I will choose the latter."

Edward was a friend of the Daniel's right from their university days, so they practically did everything together. Daniel stopped by his house. At this moment, he needed someone to tell him that he was doing the right thing, he needed someone to cheer him up and Edward seemed to be the only person that came to mind.

He felt miserable. If Nancy cared less about his decision nowadays, then he should question everything he had ever trusted. This was hell. But hey, is there something like hell anyway? He questioned rhetorically in his mind as he blindly sauntered towards Edward's living room.

He collapsed onto the couch close to the television stand. Alarmed, Edward ran to him, felt his pulse and acknowledged he was still alive, but drained. The last time he saw Daniel like this was when Nancy was admitted in the ICU, she had a major surgery five years ago that almost claimed her life. He became doubly concerned, and wondered if Daniel's despondency had anything to do with Nancy.

Daniel sobbed as he noticed Edward trying to sit him up on the sofa.

"Nancy is leaving me," he wailed.

This confirmed Edward's suspicions

Edward hugged his friend, surprised that his best friend was going through difficulties in his marriage and he knew nothing about it.

"She is now a Christian, and it's ruining our marriage."

Aha, Edward understood immediately. He knew Daniel grew up with a strong aversion for the religious. He had always seen them as hypocrites and God, a selfish deity who took delight in people's worship but did nothing to help those who worshipped. If Nancy has decided to live a religious life, then she had Daniel to contend with. This would be indeed more than the loss he experienced when he lost his parents in an auto crash, Edward estimated.

"Years back I had lived hopelessly. I lost my parents, and this same God whom they idolized so much couldn't spare either of them. They died calling that same Jesus!" He blurted his last word angrily.

"While the sun sets, and the moon begged me to look up to the sky, I didn't, I hardly slept. If I did, I didn't notice because I was tortured with the images of my parents having an auto-crash, calling His name as they gave up the ghost while on their way to a convention for the same Jesus! What kind of God is that?"

Daniel was weeping uncontrollably. "Of course I forced myself to acknowledge they were no more, and that I was alone. I wanted to believe they were still going on a trip and would come back some day. But I had to live and fulfill the promise I made to them and so the tornado of emotions was locked in my body, my soul. Every day I lived with my religious uncle and aunt reminded me of how much I hated God, so I had to do everything I could to leave there, because they were a lot worse than my parents."

Edward didn't console him, he let him cry; he let him pour out his emotions. "Everyone needs someone, I needed someone, Nancy is my someone. She filled that vacuum in my heart for so long. And now she wants to join that doom of a religion."

Edward stared in awe, he felt his friend's misery. He had always looked up to Daniel and his wife for marriage advice; if their marriage was heading to the rock, then his was doomed for sure. He and his wife did not have the solidity that both Dan and Nancy had; they could be better described as partners with benefits than a couple.

Edward heaved, this is sure going to be hard for him to handle. He patted Daniel on the back.

"My friend, I am at loss for words. I didn't expect this. But all the same, we will all pull through this. But how could Nancy make such a decision knowing fully well that you do not want to be associated with such?"

"If I have a magic wand, I would have surely lashed that madness out of her. Of course I had been brought up in the Christian faith: but that creed had become worse than useless to me since I had intellectually realized the utter inefficiency of that God and his Christian members to deal with difficult life problems. Spiritually I was adrift in chaos and reduced to want. To watch my own wife turn into that maniac is what I can't accept," He responded.

"What I went through Eddie is what I do not hope to repeat. Dealing with such emotion is hard," He continued.

"Dan my friend, at times, life gives us painful blows. We will be lost between the devil and the deep blue sea. Take things easy my friend. She will surely get to normal."

CHAPTER FOUR

you are golden

Nancy was drained. In just a matter of weeks, she had lost a lot of weight. She brushed her hair and changed into a dress her late mother made her long ago; she obviously needs a lot of new clothes. She wore a black blazer and sprinted downstairs, needing to find Daniel, who she had been calling for hours non-stop and he had not been picking up. She prayed everything was alright with him.

After long hours of riding all over town, she couldn't see Daniel, most of their friends had not seen him except for Edward who said he had left the house couple of hours before, after crying his heart out.

Nancy's car stopped at the church's premises. She met no one but the church door was open. She felt all alone. Is this really worth it? She asked herself. She was sacrificing everything she had, a happy home with her hubby all in the quest to know this God so much more. With a sudden realization, she acknowledged she couldn't question God; He was the all-knowing God after all.

She walked down to the altar, knelt before the pulpit, the emotions she had been holding up for so long finally let loose through her tears, and they freely streamed down her cheeks. She silently prayed, realizing how strong she had been these few weeks to contend with Daniel, God has been giving her strength that she never knew she had.

"You will be fine Nancy," she told herself.

"This is the time that you have to build your faith Nancy, this is a test of your faith and how much you love the God that gave you Dan as your husband. God can never let you down. I assure you that this time will surely pass and you will win Dan, not only to yourself but to God as well." She continued telling herself in consolation.

Dan was sitting outside the bar in the lounge, looking so gloomy that anyone could recognize it from a single look at his face. He sipped his drink and dropped the glass.

"You are not solving your problem this way man," He thought grimly.

He dropped a bill at the bar and pushed his way out of the premises. His phone rang, it was Nancy. He wearily ignored her call. He had not seen her since the evening he stormed out from their house. His features twisted with pain as he thought of her. Several times he'd waver, desperately wanting to return to her. Twice she had called, and when he'd finally picked, the sorrow in her voice wrenched his heart as she begged him to come home. Knowing that she will not agree to his demands, he hung up once.

Anger at the God who had caused this division between them rose in him and he cursed him under his breath. He stopped his car to enable him pay attention to what was going on in his mind.

"I just hate you this God!" He busted out.

"You should have chosen another person, not my wife for crying out loud, not my Nancy...I love you Nancy, but I can't help but feel this way over your new belief my love."

Listlessly, he continued driving and he stopped at a club, with hope that watching people dance would help him clear his thoughts of things but the club did poorly in gaining his attention. "I am going home!" He said.

Nancy heard a brisk walk down the veranda and she quickly stood up with expectation, weariness written all over her face. Daniel walked through the door, his hands steadying the slight figure with which he almost collided.

"Nancy!" he exclaimed. Startled and thinking of nothing else to say, he gave her a tight hug followed by a kiss.

When he finally left her, he felt his heart leap inside his chest, hope surging in him that everything would be alright. To him, it seemed he had been gone for ages.

"Dan I have been so worried about you! Are you alright?"

The tenderness in her voice melted the ice that had gripped his heart. He looked at her and she seemed thinner and her eyes were shadowed with deep hurt. "She has been crying for long," he said to himself.

He realized now just how much he was hurting her. He didn't respond and just stared at her. The glow in her skin was still there but the happiness on her face each time she comes to open the door for him has disappeared and in its place a weariness which he couldn't help but feel responsible for.

Nancy noticed that he had drunk all night. The pungent smell of liquor was evident on him.

"Dan, you were drinking all night? Sweetheart you shouldn't be doing this to yourself. Come with me."

She pulled him to herself, leading the way to the bedroom him. The tears came back her eyes again. She felt her husband's hands turning cold and flattened on her shoulder. Suddenly Daniel loosened his grip on her and she faltered.

"Nancy, couldn't we – couldn't you forget this? I wouldn't care that you went to church every Sunday, if you would forget the rest of the activities and programmes..." He blurted out.

Nancy's eyes widened incredulously. She wasn't expecting her Dan to have even given it a thought. Her gaze fell, she was impressed with Daniel for making effort to reconcile their differences but she now knew that being a Christian entailed more than going to church every Sunday.

"I'd do anything for you," Her voice trembled. "But darling, I can't go back to the way we were living. There wasn't any time in our lives for God."

He studied her face and thought about how drunk he sounded. Was he even honest about what he was telling her at the moment?

Surmising that Daniel needed rest and that it would be better they talked things over in the morning, she tried to scoop Dan into her tiny arms.

"Other people in our crowd go to church sometimes, some of them often, but they don't try to bring it home with them," Daniel wasn't relenting.

He just might be sober though, Nancy thought.

"But baby, we could be so much happier with Christ in our home. Even during these terrible weeks without you, I've had the first real peace I've ever known, oh Daniel! I'm not a fanatic! But what I have found is so much better than the few things I have left behind."

Dan's jaw set stubbornly. "I wouldn't even mind your not drinking or smoking. I've always respected women who didn't feel a need for cigarettes. But the way you feel about it, it wouldn't stop there. I have seen it before! I couldn't live with that kind of religion again. Please Nancy, church on Sunday and let it go at that!" He cried this part out loud in distress.

"I love you Dan but..." Nancy hesitated, "this is a better way for our salvation."

Wearily, Dan let go of her and made for the bedroom. Nancy sat on the floor, leaning against the wall. She exhaled heavily. Now what? They were becoming strangers each day and every effort was proving abortive. Things can't continue like this, she thought.

The next morning Nancy woke up feeling listless. She knew she had to make breakfast for her husband Dan, but she couldn't just get up from the bed. Her whole body ached; she felt nauseous and was at the verge of throwing up when she quickly rushed to the lavatory. Dan who saw her when she was running into the lavatory followed her. That was a familiar symptom, "Nancy is pregnant," He thought to himself. He held her warmly.

"Do you need to see our doctor?"

Blurred images floated through her mind, she recalled her discussion with Daniel, nothing concrete; they had not arrived at a conclusion. She knew she didn't need a doctor; she was pregnant and was keeping the baby.

In previous years she had murdered several of her babies. Now accepting God in her life had revealed to her how much of a sinner she had been, a terrible one. But being a God who made the unworthy worthy, she knew he had forgiven her sins and made her whole. Never again will she kill her baby.

"I am keeping the baby." She said, finding her way into the bedroom. She buried her feet into the fluffy rug on the floor. She did some kegel exercises, ignoring Daniel totally. She knew what was going on in his mind but was definitely not going to buy the idea of killing her baby again.

"Come with me, we are going to the hospital immediately, you cannot have a baby in this situation Nancy, I cannot allow it."

His face darkened as he said those words. Nancy's mouth opened in shock, she plopped to the bed. "I can't do that again."

"I insist Nancy, and we are going now. Do me the favor and go and get dressed please."

Nancy shook her head. Anger blazed in Daniel's eyes, he stared at her sternly. At least he is making effort to make the marriage work, why the hell was she not doing the same, he wondered.

"I have prayed, I have cried to God for forgiveness and the peace I feel inside only proves to me that He has forgiven me. I will not trade that peace I feel within for anything."

"Not even for me?"

Daniel asked his wife with a mild and sympathetic tone. Nancy felt her eyes tearing. He tilted his head and studied her face for a moment. He didn't wipe the tears, he let it flow.

"I thought we were done discussing this Nancy, you are my love, my life. I won't stand you doing this to us."

Nancy held his hands, she didn't want to leave this man whom she had built a life with but she had come to the realization that there was a better life in Christ. She of course did want him to change too, but how could she do it without continuing to trigger all of the hurt they both currently felt?

Daniel cupped her chin and gave her a gaze that pierced through her soul.

"We can still stop this madness and get back to the life we have been living."

In tears, she shook her head from right to left and to right again.

"Where is my Nancy? The one I love, I need her back because this one is torturing me," He screamed, getting up in fury.

"She is right here with you Daniel," Nancy responded in quiet defiance.

"She is right here," she repeated, "But changed, positively changed."

The atmosphere was becoming intense. She didn't want it to be so, at least for the sake of the child. Nancy took a deep breath and exhaled.

"We should go to the hospital, but only to know how many weeks gone I am. Daniel, we are having a baby and that's a blessing. So can we focus on that now?"

"Honey, let's make this work please."

Daniel was lost, Nancy would probably be his death, one moment she was snarling like a wounded lion, the next, soft and calm like a kitten. "Oh Nancy, kill me already." Speechless, he got up blindly and followed her.

At the hospital, Doctor Sonia confirmed she was well into her first trimester. How could that be? She felt no early symptoms of pregnancy. Sonia was bewildered when she admitted that she was going to keep the baby. Nancy told Sonia she didn't intend to toe the path of abortions anymore. Sonia was happy but curious as to why Daniel had been questionably silent all through. Sonia hadn't just been their family doctor but also a dear friend of theirs. Sonia respected their decision to keep whatever that is going on between them, she advised Nancy on some of the things she would need to do if she really wanted to keep the baby – in any case, she was already stressed enough to be in danger of having a miscarriage if she wasn't careful.

While the decision to keep the baby had still not been totally accepted by Daniel, he still felt he had to do everything possible to make sure that she is out of danger.

What should have been a moment of excitement for Nancy and her husband had been replaced with sadness, a test of her faith and her love for her husband.

She did however have love in her heart and faith in her soul; love for her husband and faith in God who had given her a second chance in life, yes a second chance - she was newly married to Daniel when she had multiple brain surgeries, she was diagnosed with brain cancer. For months she was placed on life support, fed through a tube and had several casts placed on her. But through it all, she survived.

Now, she had come into the light of God's holiness, and she was not going to back away.

Nancy sat down on the couch as they entered the living room. Daniel turned the knob and entered, trying to hide the weariness on his face.

"Why don't you go take a shower while I quickly make something for you?" He suggested to her.

She nodded absentmindedly and sprinted towards the stairs, she turned to see him glancing at her.

"I wish this trouble between us would be forgotten. I wouldn't want to raise a baby in a situation as this Nancy, let's stop this before it tears us apart." He finally bore out his mind to her.

"Daniel what is this?" The tears trailed down her cheeks. "I didn't cheat on you, I didn't steal from you, I didn't kill anyone. I only accepted Jesus Christ!"

"It would have better if you killed me Nancy."

She knelt before him and held his hand but Daniel's body shuddered in anger, he wasn't listening.

"I love you."

"But you love Jesus more; I cannot share you with him."

Forgetting that he wanted to make food for his wife, he pushed her away, ignored her tearful pleas, grabbed his car key and left the house.

Still lying on the floor, Nancy couldn't get herself up. She curled her frame, holding the fluffy rug close to the center table. A ball of tear rolled down her cheeks. She tried gathering her sanity, she just couldn't deal with the trauma all alone, was her whole world crumbling in just a twinkle of an eye, she wondered? Her head throbbed in pain, her heart ached, but immediately her palm rested on her tummy, she thought she could feel the life growing inside of her. This is a blessing of God to her, her comfort.

CHAPTER FIVE

you don't have to give up, hang in there, I am coming

Daniel didn't come home that night, in what was fast becoming a habit; he either stayed out late, or didn't come home at all. He resorted to ignoring Nancy's calls. He felt her missing him a lot might make her change her mind but despite that, he was hurting as much as she was. He kicked out the stool standing on his way and made for the door, out of the bar.

Nancy stood, seemingly lifeless on the doorway, perplexed at seeing Daniel. It had been four days since he was last home – a first in their marriage. She had come to resign herself to the inevitable. And anyways, her baby needed her to be strong.

Daniel steadied her and entered the living room.

"Should I be perplexed or excited at the fact that finally, I have come to acknowledge that the woman I have been sharing my heart with doesn't love me?"

"Where have you been honey?" she asked ignoring Daniel's question.

"In search of real peace," he replied sarcastically.

"Dan, I would give up anything for you, I will lay my life a thousand times for you but I will not give up my lord," A shaky breath escaped her lips as she reminded Daniel of her stand before he tried to persuade her further.

Disbelief showed in Dan's face, then fury, she took his hands as he turned away.

"Oh Dan, I haven't the right words – I can't make you understand, think about your life. The man that led me to Christ is in the city, this weekend. Won't you go and hear him tonight? Please, for my sake! For the sake of our baby and the love we've shared."

He jerked his hand free and stalked blindly to their bedroom. Tears streamed down Nancy's cheeks as she watched him climb the stairs without looking back.

Minutes later, Dan climbed down the stairs with his luggage. Nancy startled by what she saw, and rose in curiosity.

"Darling you are not going to do this, are you? Are you leaving the house? Our home?"

"Home? Is this home? I no longer feel okay in this place you call home, so I am leaving for you and your God to have your way. I can only ask you for one favor and that is you take care of my baby in your womb and make sure nothing happens to it, because if something happens to my child I will never forgive you."

He dragged his bags out the door and Nancy watched as he walked out, blindly colliding with the door. Her heart was in her throat, disbelief, shock and confusion whirled through her head.

"God! Am I dreaming? What is happening to my marriage, is this how you want it God? For my husband to leave me?"

She lamented all these with a teary voice, then picked up her phone and rang the pastor. She needed to speak with someone before she lost her sanity. She spoke with her pastor, pouring out her heart and emotions to him. They prayed over the phone after words of encouragement. She felt delighted that someone somewhere was still there for her – God.

That evening, Daniel threw himself on the narrow hotel bed after hours of aimlessly walking with anger ravaging him. Minutes later, his anger burned out but in its place a terrible depression gripped him. He could not live without Nancy, as he thought about her lovely face, the tenderness in her eyes when she looks at him, the way she greets everyday as a treasure to be shared with him. He groaned aloud.

"No, I cannot live without her, but she has become…"

He shuddered at the thought.

"I would rather die than watch her turn into the kind of crabbed, dry person my aunt had been. With those kind of irritating dressing of theirs, covering every single part of the body. How can one even breathe? And Nancy, wasn't she smart enough to not believe the kind of fables that they always say there? What did George even tell my wife to make her change so much into someone I can barely recognize?"

Unable to rest, he got to his feet and grimaced at the haggard face that looked back from the mirror. Perhaps a shower will clear his mind, he reasoned. He opened the bathroom door and walked in.

Refreshed by the cool water, Dan stopped, razor in mid stroke, he looked up at the white ceiling that stared back at him.

"The Nelsons were religious people but it didn't affect them neither did it cramp their lives. What was it that the Nelsons said before about getting ready for church every Sunday? If I can try that out then I and Nancy will definitely be together forever, there is nothing wrong in pretending to accept a religion just to save my marriage."

Finished with the shave, he laid back on the bed.

"I am not sure if I can be able to pretend to be a Christian but there is one thing I am sure of, I am not going to lose Nancy to that God of hers. Never!"

He dialed reception on the intercom to prepare his bill. He stood up and dressed in faded jeans and a turquoise-coloured shirt.

"I will go to church and listen to the old fables the lunatics at the altar surely must spout."

Daniel found himself stopping at the church parking lot. He took a quick glance at the church surrounding, giving a mocking smile. He could hear the choristers singing loudly and congregations singing simultaneously.

"This new evangelist will be popular judging from newspaper reports and most of the crowds attending his meetings. If he can draw that kind of crowd, he is probably an expert in wooing people."

He smiled to himself again as he entered the church, remembering how long it had been since he last attended a church service. He folded his long frame into the seat and looked about him curiously. The vast audience amazed him. Most were well dressed and from the look of things, they were intelligent people. He turned his attention to the men on the platform. They seemed cheerful and at ease. In fact, anyone of them could have been a business partner, judging from their dressing and demeanour. The music was good and Dan found himself enjoying it.

When the preliminary services were over, the evangelist stepped into the rostrum. In a firm, clear voice, he read from the Bible. Then without dramatics but with strong convictions, he sent forth his message. Dan frowned. This was no after-dinner lecture nor did it sound anything like those shabby fables he heard as a child. The man spoke with obvious authority from the scripture and Dan found himself listening because the message was appealing to him.

"...while we were yet sinners Christ died for us, he gave up his throne in heaven and came in the likeness of man for us to be redeemed. We are all sinners but now we are made a new creature if only we accept Christ as our personal Lord and savior. He is able to make you whole. He is able to set you free from the bondages of sin and guilt. The devil sentenced us to death but Jesus came with life and an abundant life for that matter, why not give him a chance to recreate you and give you an eternal peace in His glory..." The pastor preached with a piercing sincerity.

Daniel grew furious, he wanted to stay and listen to this man but something in him asked him to stand up and leave the church premises.

"The man is a good actor," He said to himself. "But I will not fall for this funny drama of his. He stood up, ignoring the eyes that suddenly turned to him and left through the exit.

He opened his car and went in and heaved a sigh of relief. He wound down his windows to drive away with the breeze blowing, as if to erase the lingering words of the preacher. He thought about Nancy and the baby she was carrying in her womb.

"Nancy has to be kidding if this kind of drama is what she fell for. Thank goodness I am out of there."

He didn't want to go back to the house, but he couldn't stop thinking about her, and the baby she was carrying.

"My baby," He moaned, "Our baby..." His heart calmed at the thought of being a father, he would not leave his baby fatherless.

It was almost evening the next day when Daniel returned home, only to see Nancy with a lady, both carrying their bibles. Nancy ran to the front door on sighting him. Daniel didn't want to talk to anybody at that particular moment. He had already figured out that the lady sitting close to the banister was Nancy's church member.

His heart ached. Nancy has moved on, he thought. He walked closer to the lady and stared at her wordlessly; he feared he would weep if he tried to speak. Annabel stood up in surprise.

"Honey, Annabel and I were just having moments with God."

"I know," Daniel replied before Nancy could say another word. Annabel rose to leave.

"Not so soon miss, are you done with your chit chat? Just so you know, the god you people are so proud of doesn't exist." He said, making his mockery apparent.

"It's enough Daniel, you..."

"Shut up Nancy! You are falling for the hallucinations of mortals and you think I will be happy with that?"

He turned to the woman now. "What are you still doing in my house, you bundle of lies?! Get out!" Annabel ran out in fear.

"And you Nancy, I came back because I want us to be together. Forget about your religion Nancy, I am the religion which you must follow. I am your husband, your love and even your god. I am you and you are me! For crying out loud Nancy is it not obvious that I want us, I love you..."

"If you love me then accept my new faith! I can no longer live in darkness for I have found light Daniel."

He laughed hysterically.

"Oh, I see...I am darkness huh? Nancy the man who gave you his first love and life is darkness right?"

"That is not what I meant Daniel..."

"Damn your God!"

Nancy slapped her husband as he uttered the words.

Daniel looked at her with his left palm on his cheek. Nancy broke down in tears; she wasn't expecting that, Daniel wasn't expecting it too.

"This is religion too huh? You had never done this before no matter how enraged you were."

"I am sorry... this is to tell you how much I have grown with God. I am so sorry honey, I couldn't bear hearing you say those words against God, I..." she knelt down weeping.

"I thought seeing you today will bring us back again. It is okay Nancy; tell me when you are ready to file for a divorce."

Those words pierced through her soul, what was Daniel talking about? He could not be serious.

"No! Do not do this, Daniel I beg of you, you want my child to grow up without a father? Is that what you want for her? I am sorry I slapped you, I am sorry for all I've said. Please I am begging you Daniel...let's just put this into consideration and give this a deeper thought."

"We have been the best of couples and even the envy of your friends. Why is this happening? Why does the devil want to use you and your blindness to break us apart...Please reconsider your decision over this matter, there is always a way to a new beginning please," she pleaded.

"I cannot go back on my decision and that is final, I am leaving but make sure you take care of my baby. I will still be providing for you till our divorce is made official; then, I can divide my asset for the sake of my child. Take care, Nancy."

A tear trickled down the corner of her eye and traveled down her temple.

Daniel came down from the stairs, he glanced at Nancy who seemed to be drenched in tears; he pecked her on the cheek. Her delicate hands grabbed his, the appeal in her teary eyes wanted to stop him but he looked away, withdrew his hands and made for the door. Nancy watched him as he opened the door and walked away gently. She broke down crying out her heart and praying amid tears.

"God, this is too much for me. My life has been shattered in the twinkle of an eye; I am at the feet of your cross... have mercy on me and bring back my husband for me. I cannot stay without him, oh my God, he is my world and the father to the baby you have given to us. Why me? Please do not tempt me with this God because I will backslide... I will die of depression my God please bring Daniel back to me."

CHAPTER SIX

every time you cry, I feel it

Nancy couldn't breathe. Her heart ached, her body ached too, and her dry mouth kept calling on Daniel. He had promised to protect her and stand by her forever no matter what, but right now that forever seemed a facade.

She screamed in utter despair as she reminisced about her past. It was then she felt something being torn apart in her stomach; she screeched and her vision became hazy. She clutched the skin close to her pelvis. She prayed her baby would stay. Her throat was only capable of whimpering; "Jesus...Jesus, Jesus."

She gasped for air. She tried gathering up strength - her baby will not die. With all the strength in her, she reached for her mobile phone. Annabel won't be too busy today. She dialed Annabel, who luckily gave her a prompt response.

Nancy was in the hospital; she had passed out when Annabel was driving her down to Doctor Sonia's hospital. Fortunately for her, her baby was fine.

She regained consciousness; Sonia called her into the consulting room. She wouldn't have stepped off the hospital bed till she heard that her baby was still in shape. She blessed her stars on hearing the news.

"Mrs. Daniel, what is happening to you?"

That was the question Sonia asked as she stepped into her office.

Mrs. Daniel? She should take glory of the name till Daniel makes their divorce official.

Sonia noticed that from the look of things, all wasn't well with her once cheerful patient, the woman whose marriage she admired. "Your baby is okay for now but I am afraid if care is not taken you are going to lose this pregnancy."

"Nancy..." she held her hand now, "I've been your doctor for years now and I know you and Daniel very well as a happy couple. What happened to you people? What happened to the humor I always see in your eyes? Are you going through hard times in your marriage with Daniel? I am your doctor but I can also be your friend. Please for the sake of this unborn child..."

A shaky breath escaped her lips. She needed to summon enough courage to speak candidly with Sonia.

"Doctor, as it stands now, my baby is the only one I have. She is going to be my world and life. I will live for her. Daniel and I have separated, just for some time."

She briefed her story, but Sonia wasn't having it.

"You almost had a miscarriage and that is dangerous considering how far gone you are. Daniel is too enlightened to even think thought of leaving you at this critical stage of your life. But whatever the problem is, you have to pull through this Nancy, your baby needs you."

"I am sorry to hear this Nancy. You know, when you think of someone as the pillar of your entire world, that's when they crush you. I might not know what went wrong between you two but know that you are strong and you will overcome this. I am here for you always Nancy. Don't make the mistake of forgetting to call me when you need someone else. I would abduct you and you will stay with me until you and David patch things up."

They both laughed and for a moment, she felt relieved of the burden that lay on her heart.

"Thank you so much doctor for your kind words. I am a bit relieved now, thank you so much."

Sonia hugged her tightly. She understood what she was going through because she had been there before.

"God will give you the strength to move on, dear. Here are your medications and you should be going now to get some rest. You really need it." She told Nancy, handing over a bag of pills to her. Nancy thanked Sonia and headed home.

Daniel stumbled into his small rented apartment. He had made a life decision and it made him wonder if he would ever get over the consequences that would follow.

He brought out his phone and went through the numerous text messages Nancy had sent him. He had to blink a few times to get his eyes focused on the bright light from the screen.

"I hope you are safe and sound Daniel, God loves you. You can come home to Him, to me and to our baby."

Why couldn't she just send a message and leave God out of it for once? He kept deleting her messages, the ones with God in them.

He thought of her, her soft lips, her deep brown eyes, her slender but curvy frame.

Goodness really blessed Nancy, he said to himself. He thought of the baby she was carrying, who was it going to look like?

He wished the baby would look like him so that the resemblance will haunt Nancy, making it impossible to live without him. He smiled at that, then frowned on realizing how badly he was hurt and was still hurting.

God is a damn liar. He promised everything to be good then he breaks his promise. He dozed off cursing God under his breath.

Months dragged by, Nancy accepted her fate. She did miss her husband but she believed that whatever the future holds is best. She thought of how far she had gone, what she had left behind and how Daniel came into her life shortly after the death of her mother.

She remembered how sick she was on the hospital bed where she fought for her life but lost to death. Her cheating father left them for his mistress, in fact all through their lives, they lived in misery. Her father bullied her mother; they'd go for days without food. As if not bad enough, her father stole from her mother, money she made from her petty business. Her home was hell, but her mother always had the right words to say to her to make sure she didn't give up on life. When things became too rough to handle, her mother said things to cheer her up. She remembered her feeble hands in hers when she was wasting away on a hospital bed. What was it that she always said to her?

"Everything happens for a reason, do not give up. All these just make you stronger."

She was a woman par excellence, except for the fact that she was a fool for love, she had her convictions but her world revolved around her monster of a husband, Nancy thought. Her mother was resilient, hardworking, loving and caring to a fault and she gave her life up for someone she loved, trying to make ends meet and never bothered about the cancerous growth in her lung. Nancy took after her mother, except for the fact that her own convictions were high, and she went for it. She had lost Daniel because of those convictions.

Daniel was the only man that stood by her when she was in shreds. He picked her up and watched her grow into the woman she was now. She heaved. Life is depressingly funny.

Closing her eyes, she took a deep breath and gave herself a few moments to gather her composure. She was already nine months gone. She should expect the kicking of her little girl any moment so she made sure to keep people around her.

That evening, the heavens opened wide and it rained heavily. The ponderous downpour was accompanied by booming thunder. Nancy wondered why it was raining this heavily by the end of September. She had already packed her bag to go to the hospital. She looked all around the room; her gaze fell on Daniel's portrait on the wall.

"Wherever you are, we are having our baby, I hope you are safe."

She knew it had been months already, Daniel had even stopped replying her texts and taking her calls but her prayers had always been with him. Maybe not to come back to her but for his ways to be inclined with the purpose of God for his life. He had made so many enemies by duping people and not having any remorse about it, so right now, all that Nancy cared about was his life - he shouldn't die in sin. She still had that love for him somewhere in her heart but for some reason, she feels Daniel now hates her. Besides the Bible says, "Everyone will hate you on account of my name. But whoever stands firm until the very end shall be saved." That was the very hope of her existence.

A month after their separation, she had loaned money from the bank and started up an online store. Till date, she had been using the profit to foot her bills. She hoped to get a job once she has weaned her baby. Her plans for the future had already been laid out, she had friends from church, the pastor was there for her, Sonia too and even Daniel's friends. Her head throbbed of thinking how her life has changed from moments of misery to moments of grace and how grateful she was for living it with God's wisdom. George who led her to Christ relocated almost immediately after her conversion. She smiled.

She staggered down the stairs holding her small suitcase, she dialed Annabel and the number seemed unreachable. Her head throbbed again. Network was definitely poor this evening, she kept dialing Annabel all to no avail. Having no other option, she had to put the phone on fixed redial mode.

She felt her baby coming. "Was Annabel never coming? What is wrong with the network anyway? Oh God not today," she cried helplessly.

She felt the kicking of her girl inside, she hissed in pain. The twisting and stabbing pain ripped her whole being. What was it that Sonia said about being in labor?

Breathe, catch your breath and breathe hard. She gasped for air.

"The devil...is a liar," she told her baby, gritting her teeth.

She whimpered in pain, shook her head and caught her breath one more time; being alone is taking its toll on her right now. Her shaking hands reached for her phone, it appears Annabel would never come. She dialed Sonia, and it rang immediately.

"I am in labour," she cried out to Sonia immediately she answered the phone.

Annabel and their pastor paced through the hospital premises. Nancy needed them, at least someone she could talk to and share her joy with after delivery. They couldn't let her think that Daniel was still around, though it's inevitable. They watched the nurses move back and forth through the glass doors. Confusion and worry plastered themselves on Pastor Gabriel's face when he saw a group of doctors and nurses race inside. His eyes fell on Nancy, watching her face contort in pain. He shut his eyes and prayed to God- He shouldn't let anything bad happen to these children of his. Let Nancy be among the Hebrew women that delivers with no complications.

Annabel and Pastor Gabriel sprang up from the couch they were lying on the second they heard the cry of a baby. They grinned widely - God was indeed faithful.

Nancy couldn't take her eyes off her; it was like watching her past meet her present. She was an exact replica of Daniel. She smiled amid her thoughts, at that moment; she missed Daniel who seemed to be gone forever.

"We are going to pull through," she said silently in her heart. "You will be my Princess and I, your queen and king." She carried her baby and pecked her cheeks.

Before Pastor Gabriel could enter the ward to see Nancy, he was called out separately by Doctor Sonia. The stressed face she wore made Pastor Gabriel wonder if everything was alright.

"Tell me what happened doctor, is she okay? What about the baby? Are they alright?" Panic was etched on Gabriel's face as he entered the consulting room.

She smiled.

"Yes, she gave birth to a beautiful baby girl. Congratulations!"

"Thank you very much doctor, and may God bless you for the work you have done." The Pastor was obviously joyous.

Annabel shouted for joy as she entered the room with Pastor Gabriel, the expression knew no bounds, she carried the tiny baby in her palms and congratulated her dear friend. "Her name is Gloria." Nancy said out loud.

"Wow, such a lovely name for a happy child." Annabel said.

"Yes, today is one of the happiest days of my life, I am grateful to God and to you all. You people have been the source of my strength and my reason to keep living. Thank you all." Nancy expressed her gratitude with a large smile on her face.

"It is God that we owe the thanks and we will keep thanking him for that, it is well with our souls."

CHAPTER SEVEN

***I feel every ounce of your pain, and I am sorry"

Daniel came back after spending months in the United Kingdom. His fears were that everything would remind him of Nancy, and the thought of staying in the same country without seeing her, hurt him so much. He abandoned his work and friends all for the fear of running into Nancy someday.

He thought being a Casanova would help him get over Nancy and ruin his love for her but he always ended up comparing the women he met with her- his beautiful Nancy.

It was morning once again and Daniel was greeted by a fair lady that came out from his bedroom. He took a deep look at her and pretended not to hear the greeting but rather asked rudely;

"When are you leaving my house Selene?"

"Are we going to keep dragging this issue on and on? Where do you want me to go? Are you expecting another woman in this house Daniel? Because if you are, I will not let you. We have been together for days now and you want me to leave your house just like that? What did I do to you?" She asked calmly.

"The question is, what didn't you do?" He asked Selene, annoyed.

"You are here to help me get my wife out of mind, yet you've failed to help with that. And madam, this is my house and I am no longer comfortable with you in it. I have a wife and I want to go back to her, because she needs me. I think she is already due to give birth. I do not want to handle you like a whore and that's why I am pleading with you amicably to leave my house."

He closed his eyes, his hands on his face. Just mere admitting that she was still his wife brought back memories. He wished there was something he could do to wash all those sadness, the sorrow, the nightmares away. He needed to heal badly.

"So I am now a whore to you? You did not know I was a whore when you brought me into your house abi?"

"You came into my house with your flimsy excuses. I did not willingly bring you in to my abode so please mind your words. I am just giving you till this evening. I do not want to come back here and meet you in this house tonight."

"Are you not afraid to be with a man that is not ready to marry you? Have you ever asked yourself what you really want for yourself? Because I asked myself that question and still cannot get an answer as to what I am doing with you. You are going to live for nothing and maybe die for nothing." He said, almost contemptuously.

"You said the rain resembles new beginning to you right?" He asked, hysterically.

"Yes." she answered after a moment, puzzled.

"It's dropping really hard outside, get a life! Our chapter has been closed." He left, leaving Selene to her thoughts.

Selene felt sad all of sudden. The only mystery that has kept Daniel's goodness from showing is his wife, she thought to herself. There are some good and bad things one can't wash away, and Nancy is one of the bad things he can't wash away.

That evening, Daniel sat on the chair gulping his drink and watching the television set before him. The presenter was a preacher and was taking time to explain the word of God from every chapter he quoted. He found himself listening to him.

He thought aloud to himself, "How can one change so blindly over what another man is saying? What would they have told Nancy to make her change so much?"

He took a closer look at the man on the television.

"What will this man ever tell me to make me change my personality? He is just like me. He applied a little make up just to look good to his audience, is that Biblical? Is that not worldly? He is doing it to entice his congregation and lure young women into temptation. I can vividly recall that their Bible admonishes that Religious people should not be of the world, whatever happened to those godly principles and Biblical injunctions?"

He sighed, images of Nancy appearing on his face. The thought of her made him drowsy and he stood up to leave. As he made for the door, he almost collided with Nick, their family friend who was about entering the bar. They stared at each other in bewilderment but finally gave each other a warm hug.

"So you are still on the surface of the earth, where have you been man?" Nick asked, giggling. Daniel followed him back to the bar.

"I have been here and there, my friend. It is just that my work and other activities do not afford me with enough time to come around anymore," he responded.

Nick observed his friend. He seemed rather drunk. The Daniel he used to know was jovial and had a great aura around him. Although he had some dubious dealings with associates, he still extended his hands to the poor and needy. With Nancy, they were the one of the more admirable couples in town.

"Have you seen your baby yet? Nancy gave birth months ago."

The news sounded more like cold water had been poured on Daniel. For a moment he felt lost in his thoughts, absentmindedly stroking his arm - it was his baby after all. He couldn't deny the fact that he was a father. He imagined how beautiful the baby would be, his Nancy was beautiful and he himself, reasonable handsome. He smiled at the thought. Then with sudden surge of realization, he was sad knowing that he had asked Nancy to abort the baby "I'll go and see them." he thought.

He stood up, shaking hands with Nick and apologizing for not staying to catch up with him. He had a lot of things on his mind, - claiming his paternity being one of them, the rest will fall into place.

It was a Saturday, and Daniel could not help but stop over at the house where he and Nancy built memories that he found hard to erase. He got out of the car and took a brief stop at his gate. He admired the serenity and tranquility of the compound he used to call his own; the place where he built the foundation of his life. He took a walk around the compound, reminiscing how life used to be there with him and Nancy.

After admiring the compound, he gathered his breath then knocked on the door. After knocking for a long time without any response, he opened the door and tiptoed into the living room only to meet Nancy sitting on the couch with Gloria lying beside her. He grew numb while Nancy stared at him. He slowly walked towards them, nervous to his stomach. It was as if his soul was about to be detached from his body.

That baby…that was him. Conflicting emotions coursed through him: should he cry? Should he smile? Should he go and grab the baby from Nancy?

Time stood still. Gulping with difficulty, Nancy leaned up on her toes.

He stared into her eyes, those eyes that exuded so much love; those eyes he often drowned in had now been replaced with so much pain. His lips parted slightly and he took a step closer.

Nancy put her palm on his face, motioning him not to step closer. An air of betrayal filled the atmosphere and Nancy started to feel intensely sad. She wanted to reach out to him but she held back, she had been preparing for this day, the words, the actions were all planned out but here she was, fumbling. "Calm down Nancy, you are in control." She told herself.

She let out a breath that she didn't realize she was holding.

"I was knocking..." Daniel said in almost a whisper

"Yes, you were."

"And... you didn't open the door?"

"I knew who was knocking."

All the emotions that filled the room dissolved, what had transpired between them flashed on their faces. "Go straight to the reason why you are here, Daniel."

It wasn't a plea, it was a command. He had no right to show up here and pretend nothing happened. She needed to hear him out, she mulled. He needed to explain himself.

Daniel bent towards where the baby laid and took a long look at her, held her tiny fingers and kissed it. "I came for her, I came for my baby."

It was like a sword pierced through her heart, she gathered her composure."What nonsense are you talking about Daniel? Do you have a child?"

"Yes, I do. I have a child and she is my flesh and blood. Do you want to deny me my paternity right Nancy? I can sue you for that you know..."

"Are you not ashamed of yourself? Are you not ashamed to even claim that this baby is yours? Do you even know how she came into this world? You were away living your life while I was in excruciating pains. You have the effrontery to come in here to call my baby your daughter?"

Her words revealed her pain. She couldn't hide the incredulity in her voice too.

"What are you trying to say here? That I abandoned you and my child? Are you trying to put the whole blame on me? I tried to make us stay but you preferred your God to me. Please Nancy do not open old wounds."

Images of the pain she went through flashed in her eyes. The nerve, the nerve that Daniel had; to come into her house, and blame her for letting their marriage crash.

"Old wounds you say? Believe me Daniel when I say you have no idea about wounds."

She sat on the sofa, carrying her baby. She couldn't utter words anymore; she found comfort in her silence. Daniel stood there, not knowing what to do but he needed to make it clear to Nancy that he wants his baby.

"Anytime I think about you, I feel rage. I do not know if it is rage for the God who separated us or rage for you because you chose him over me."

"I tried to make you reason and see things in a clearer perspective. But no! You are such an egotist that you cannot let go of pride and reason calmly, and need I remind you that Jesus doesn't crash marriages, He didn't crash our marriage, your ego did."

"I will come back, and I will take my baby with me."

He left the house.

Nancy sobbed. Just when it seemed that all trouble had been forgotten, Daniel showed up, all for what? To take Gloria away from her? She probably wouldn't survive that, she thought.

The soft rays of the morning sun penetrated the windows, providing just enough light for Nancy to see the beautiful face of Gloria. She imagined life without Gloria and the possibility of losing her to her ex-husband. That was her worst nightmare. Her life would be empty.

"Oh God, Do not let this happen." she prayed briefly.

She thought about all the plans she had for Gloria, her plans of watching her grow, watching her pray, watching her recite her school rhymes, watching her run about the house happily. She thought of being called a mother, how it was one of her greatest fears, but now, a blessing she will cherish for the rest of her life.

She was awoken from her thoughts by the ringing of the doorbell, hoping Daniel had not come back again.

She rose, determined to fight it off with Daniel but was relieved on seeing Annabel. She let her in.

"Why the long face Nancy?"

"He came to see the baby. He came to claim his paternity right over my baby, Daniel came." she told Annabel as both plopped on the sofa.

"And what did you tell him?"

She was silent; apparently she didn't know what to do. Daniel had as much right over Gloria as she did. She couldn't say the baby wasn't Daniel's. That would mean she committed adultery. She was left at his mercy.

"I cannot let him do that to me."

She held her hand. "Nancy my dear, it is going to be well. Everything will work out well at the end and our God will take all the Glory."

Nancy felt tears streaming down her cheeks. When will all be well exactly?

"I thought I had forgotten about him, I didn't know that the wound was still there. It hurts. It hurts because I still love him. Yes! I still love my husband. These past months I just managed to live without him, his presence again showed me that he was still there in my heart. But his intentions for coming back were not good. Daniel has not changed one bit, he is still that same old Daniel who will stop at nothing till he gets what he wants. What am I supposed to do?"

Annabel sighed. "And that is the intention of God for you. He never intended that you will forget your husband just like that. Divorce is not the will of our God, He wants every marriage to last and stay forever under His guidance and will for his children. Please be strong, the tide will turn and you will rejoice okay? Stay strong for your baby, dear."

Nancy continued, "Daniel was like a puzzle that needed to be solved, I was his completeness, but I completed him wrongly. I supported his every action regardless of how good or bad it was. I was hoping that the goodness in him will help me win him over to God, but it's too late. Daniel is damaged already and it hurts that I was a part of that. It hurts Annabel, it hurts right here." She wept, holding her heart.

"Maybe it's not for you to change him. It is between him and God, people like that need a personal encounter with God just like apostle Paul. Stop crying dear, your baby needs you. We need you."

She wiped her tears and gave a faint smile.

"Yes, thank you. I do not know what I would have done without you. Thank you so much for being there for me and Gloria."

"It is okay my dear, in the meantime; let's get you something to eat okay?"

Nancy nodded.

During the evening of that Saturday, Daniel was perturbed as to whether he was doing the right thing. His conscience was haunting him; he wasn't there when Nancy needed him the most, and now he wanted to claim paternity rights over a baby that Nancy gave birth to. He sighed, he still loved her despite all that had happened and he could proudly say that Nancy loves him back despite what he had made her go through. But he can't be a weakling. If claiming his rights over his baby will make him close to Nancy, then he would.

After nibbling on some snacks and browsing through the evening paper, he grabbed his car keys and left his small apartment.

He stopped over at Edward's. It had been months since the last day they met, he felt they had some catching up to do. Edward screamed on seeing his dear friend. Then he frowned, asking why he left suddenly, and without a trace.

Daniel replied with a laugh, he told Edward that his business was at stake, and that it was why he came.

"I've seen my baby girl, she is beautiful." He grinned.

Edward smiled with him "Christy told me, congratulations man."

"Eddie, Nancy might not let me see her as often as I wish."

He sighed on remembering his encounter with Nancy earlier.

"Eddie, leaving Nancy was like leaving life. She was my life. In her I found the touch of love and we lived like a destined couple for years. Every day of our life was just like we newly met... how do you expect me to act when my life is about to be taken away from me? I fought for it, I cried for it and I begged for it. But the God who brought the division between us is far stronger than I am. I cannot be cowering in this town pretending that I am fine when I was not. I was dying every day, the town reminded me of Nancy and I wanted to forget her so my only option was to leave before I lost my sanity and did something drastic.

But now, I have a reason to stay back. She is acting weird, trying to deny me my paternity rights."

"Deny you your paternity right? That's ridiculous," he chuckled. "I mean who doesn't know that you are the father of the baby? Anyway, I do not doubt the power of a woman. They can do and undo, so my friend I advise you to act fast if really you want the baby. Just like she had said, one day you might wake up to realize that she has run away with your child."

Daniel glared at him.

"Look man, I am not saying that it is going to happen but look at what happened between both of you. You do not trust women. I do not trust my wife either because anything can happen." He added the last statement, laughing naughtily.

"Religion is a curse you know. When I saw her, I wanted to run to her, touch her and kiss her, just like reuniting with a loved one, but the hate was still there. My parents were strong religious people, strong to the point where every word was about Jesus. My mom would want me to participate in every activity in church when I was young. If I complained, she would tell me that Jesus had done a lot for me and if I don't reciprocate, it's a sin. But the truth of the whole thing is, that Jesus caused nothing but trouble. I hate him!"

Edward stared in bewilderment as he watched his friend pour out his hurt. He patted Daniel at the back and encouraged him to get a grip on his emotions.

CHAPTER EIGHT

you can't take what's mine, I don't want what's yours

On Tuesday afternoon, Nancy was dressing her baby up for a walk. The weather was sunny and the street, calm. She hoped that seeing happy faces and cheerful laughter would help relieve the stress she had felt the past couple of days.

Startled by the urgent knock on the door, she placed Gloria carefully on her seater and walked to check who was knocking. Two unfamiliar faces showed up, she greeted them. They flashed their identification cards; Lawyers.

Her heart jumped – Daniel was finally suing her.

The gentlemen introduced themselves and admitted that it was Daniel who sent them. Nancy was calm. She didn't know for sure why they were in her house.

"Here is a legal document we will like you to peruse," One of them said. He handed a clipped sheaf of papers to Nancy who took it and opened it hastily. After a quick scanning through the papers placed therein, she smiled. The lawyers looked at her with undisguised curiousity. Nancy closed the file and placed it on the side-stool beside her chair.

"I am not taking my baby away from her father. Daniel is the father and everyone knows that." she said calmly.

"Thank you for the brilliant comprehension of what you just read. And Yes! Our mission here is to make you understand that you are not going to deny my client his paternity right over his daughter or try to run with her," said one of the lawyers.

Nancy chuckled. "The thought never crossed my mind, Barrister. I am a Christian and I cannot stoop so low to demean my own faith... I've fought, I have no strength to fight anymore, especially with Daniel, Jesus will fix it."

"That's the more reason why you have to sign ma'am, to make our client believe that you are a Christian." They grinned.

Nancy however wondered if it was possible to run away from everything with Gloria, to somewhere safe where Daniel would not see them again. That would be a fair punishment knowing how much he's hurt them, she thought.

"And if I refuse to sign?"

"Well, that is what my client is afraid of. You see, you need to calm down ma'am. We are not taking your baby away. The essence of signing this is to erase every doubt whatsoever. Daniel has legal right over the baby, in the eyes of the law and even the God you worship, he is the father. Any other movement contrary to this gentle way of settling this doubt will attract court action and I am not too sure that you will win ma'am even though you are the mother. My candid advice is that you should sign those documents please." Chris, one of the lawyers spoke expansively.

"I will sign it, just to prove him wrong but I will not do that today... I will consult my own lawyer and Daniel would also have to be present.

He is claiming paternity from a distance..." She paused, looking at their expression.

"I do not see any reason why you have to consult your own personal lawyer, if there are terms that you want my client to know before signing it, we will put a call through and all will be settled and fine."

Nancy perused the papers again and signed. Then she handed the papers onto Chris.

"I have signed." She told them resignedly.

Her expression changed, - was there any chance of starting all over with Daniel? Signing the papers just gave him the privilege of seeing them at his own benevolence. And with that, she feared what might happen.

"There is no need to become too emotional ma'am. You still have your baby and everything is still yours." Chris assured her. They rose to leave and Nancy saw them out.

Sunday morning came and while dressing up, Nancy glanced at her wrist-watch and gasped. She was late for church and she had not dressed Gloria. She applied a little gloss on her lips, packed her hair into a messy bun and rushed out to Gloria's room. If she didn't hurry, they would surely miss the preliminary services, she thought.

She hastily opened Gloria's wardrobe and began gathering her garments. She stopped as she turned to look at Gloria, she was lying motionless. The blanket she covered her with was now stained with clots of blood. Gloria smiled sadly, her delicate fingers turned pale. Nancy looked at her lips, they were soaked with blood. Fear gripped Nancy; she flung the clothes away and ran to her baby, confused and in panic.

"Jesus! Gloria!" She screamed in fear.

Nancy suddenly found herself dazed. First, she rubbed her eyes to be sure she was not dreaming. With a sudden surge of strength, she carried Gloria and ran downstairs, muttering prayers as she went down the stairs.

"Gloria there is no divination that will ever work against you. No enchantment whatsoever! You are a daughter of Zion. I am proclaiming life and healing upon you..."

She stole a glance at her, Gloria was going still... Nancy broke down in tears. "Gloria what are you trying to do to mummy? You are not going to die, you will live for me. Wake up!"

Her car stopped over at the hospital. Thankfully, Sonia was already there. They took Gloria from her and beckoned on her to keep calm. Her tears couldn't stop, she was wailing and praying. She dialed Annabel and her Pastor and informed them of the situation. They promised her that they would be at the hospital in no time.

Gloria was immediately taken to the ICU, and specialists began to carry out examinations on her.

In the consulting room, Nancy was weeping uncontrollably; Pastor Gabriel and Sister Annabel were consoling and attempting to reassure her.

When the doctor entered, Nancy stood up eagerly and walked towards her direction.

"Don't you dare tell me I have lost my daughter, Sonia." Nancy was expectedly not going to be reasoned with at the moment in time.

The doctor held her and placed her on a seat, before joining her side, and taking a deep breath. "I am waiting!" Nancy exclaimed impatiently.

"Your baby is not dead! Calm down Nancy," Sonia began calmly.

"Well what is wrong with her then?"

The doctor stared deeply at the pastor and nodded.

"She... she is just sick."

"Of what, eh? Doesn't the sickness have a name? What is wrong with my daughter?" At this point, she had ramped up the hysteria and the fear in her voice rose up with anger.

"Alright, alright! Your daughter has cancer-Leukemia."

The ensuing silence was deafening.

"I'm sorry Nancy, she has leukemia and we have to act fast to source for the best possible way to get another bone marrow to replace her abnormal one..."

Nancy stood up confused, realizing she had no reason for standing; she tried to sit again but missed her seat and fell on the floor. Down there, she felt the heaviness of the whole world on her shoulders. Annabel who was already in tears helped Sonia to lift Nancy and make her sit.

"It is a lie, please carry out another test on her. I beg you," she said amid tears.

"Come on Nancy, do you think I would have given such a diagnosis without checking multiple times? I am hundred percent sure of what I am telling you Nancy, She was born that way."

"How did she get affected with leukemia? I am not leukemic, Daniel is not leukemic... there is no trace of that in our gene, how come my baby is leukemic?" Her exasperation grew.

"You might not be, but unwittingly, you might have done something to damage her leukocyte when she was still forming in the womb..."

"I did not do anything to have that happen to my Gloria," she interrupted.

"Were you not a smoker?"

Nancy bent her head in sorrow and despair. "Is this nemesis? Oh gracious Lord," she wailed.

"Leukemia is a blood cancer; it can be inherited or caused by environmental factors which include chemotherapy, smoking and ionizing radiation. This things damage the white blood cells without you knowing and there are chances of passing infection from a smoking mother to a ..."

"I am killing my baby? My past is haunting me and they want my baby as a sacrificial lamb? Pastor, the blood of Jesus washes away sins and iniquities of the world; will it be different with me?" She interrupted again.

"Calm down Nancy, the chances of saving your baby is high my dear. We can get a bone marrow transplant."

Annabel held her. She was weeping.

"It is possible with faith and treatment," Sonia assured her.

"I am tired... can I take my baby with me? I want to leave."

"No, you cannot. We will be monitoring her till we find a donor." Sonia said.

She rose and ran away, the doctor, Pastor and Annabel called out to her but she ignored them. "I knew this would happen someday, Jesus fix it." Pastor Gabriel said.

He shook his head in dismay and walked away.

"Doctor, I will make sure that I calm her down. Getting devastated will not proffer solutions to the problem. I will be back to check on the baby," Annabel assured.

"That's okay, we will try our best but God has the final say."

Nancy arrived at her house the evening of what had fast become a tragic day to her. She stood, feeling the emptiness of her house, how solemn everywhere was, and how much pain she was going through. She walked towards the portrait of Jesus hanging on the wall with the inscription: "by his stripes, we are healed." After taking a close look at the frame, she pulled it from the wall and smashed it on the ground, screaming at the top of her voice.

"It's a lie! You hate me, I believed in you. You should have inflicted me with any disease whatsoever and left my baby alone. What did she do to you? You gave her to me and you still want to take her away from me!"

She rolled on the floor in distress.

"I want my baby to live; take my life and leave her for me I beg you... take my life and leave Gloria for me. She is my world," she wept uncontrollably.

"I thought you wash away sins and guilt of the world, eh? I thought you renewed lives. Was that all a lie? My past is supposed to be clean because I found you. It shouldn't haunt me because they say that in you is life; that life is the salvation of mankind. Why me? Why did you choose Gloria?"

Victoria entered the house – she saw the smashed picture and Nancy, sprawled hopelessly on the floor.

"Is this the way forward? You are giving the devil the opportunity to laugh over you. This the time for you to build your faith and trust more in the ability of God's supremacy."

Nancy gathered herself up and looked straight into the eyes; her eyes revealing the hurt she was feeling.

"God? God! Build my faith in a God inflicting me with unflinching pains ever since I surrendered my life to him? Build my faith in a God who made me lose my husband, build my faith in a God who made me feel miserable, build my faith in a God who wants to take away my baby from me?"

"Shut up! Please. God can never hurt His own; he sets out to watch over us rather than hurt us." Victoria retorted.

"Oh yeah? Well then he was supposed to watch over my marriage, he watched my marriage run into ruins although I was faithful to him. He has broken me, and just like that, it seems I am losing everything."

"He will break and mold you." Victoria said softly.

Nancy interrupted her friend's attempts at making her feel better.

"Please leave. I want to be alone."

"I will let you cool off a bit but I will be back."

She left the house, leaving Nancy all alone. She felt miserable. Life, she thought, had never been fair to her. First it was Daniel, now, Gloria.

"I do not want to live without my baby. It is all over now - Daniel was right anyway. All of these are mere fables and illusions. There has been no God, no religion and no faith; every man is just a solitary being carrying his own cross. If the God that I have believed in so much cannot even spare me of my punishments then what is there to worship? Nothing! Absolutely nothing!"

CHAPTER NINE

sometimes all we need is that one friend

Monday morning, Daniel's eyes were fixed on the files in front of him. He had a lot to do. The past few weeks had not been easy so he decided to get himself together and deal with work because duties were already piling up.

He had been staring at the same page for twenty minutes, absorbing nothing. The secretary walked in to the office to tell him of a call that came in earlier.

"Yes Doris, you wanted to speak to me. Go on," he asked.

"Sir, a lady called around past nine this morning, she said she is a doctor calling from Royalty hospital..."

Daniel closed the file he was reviewing, immediately perturbed. Why would Sonia call his office?

"She said your attention is required immediately at the hospital. Your daughter was admitted there yesterday."

Startled, Daniel rose from his seat.

"What? When did she call you?"

"Thirty minutes ago, Sir."

"And you are telling me now?" He barked, injecting the irritation into his voice.

"You were busy Sir" She answered, lowering her gaze.

Sucking in his lower lip in anger, he said, "Tell Roland to prepare my car. He will continue with the servicing tomorrow, be quick."

Unpleasant images rose in his mind, he pictured Nancy being hospitalized. She was hospitalized years back and he couldn't deal with it but now...His heart ached. He hoped that his daughter was alright.

Daniel barged into Sonia's office. She was at her desk, glancing through the case files for the day. She looked up on seeing Daniel.

"Daniel," she greeted.

"What happened to my baby? Where is she?"

"Calm down please, she is fine... I mean she will definitely be fine if we act quickly."

That did not help his continuously rising anxiety.

"What are you trying to say? That my child is at the point of death?"

"I know Nancy would not have the courage to tell you, and that is the reason I called your office. You see, your daughter has leukemia."

"That is not possible," He said in disbelief. "How did you come up with that ridiculous diagnosis?"

"If some things in medical procedures should be doubted, it is because the symptoms are not certain. I am sorry Mr. Daniel but if you doubt the result of the biopsy test carried out on her please check another hospital," she said, losing patience at the constant questions about her competence.

"So, are you trying to say that she will undergo chemotherapy? She is just a baby, come on!

He bowed his head in dismay.

"She can also undergo transplant."

"Bone marrow transplant?" Daniel stood up, distraught. "I want to see her please."

"Okay."

They were about leaving the office when Daniel mentioned Nancy.

"Nancy ought to be here."

"She is heartbroken and I understand that. You needed to have seen the hurt in her eyes when she heard the news. I hope she is safe."

The doctor opened the door, Gloria was lying down. Daniel moved closer to her and sat close to her bed rubbing her curly, silky hair.

"I wish to share your pains my love."

Tears dropped from his eyes. "I do not want you to be this way. Whatever happens to you little angel, remember we have not had a father-daughter moment yet, so you are going nowhere."

He turned and looked at the doctor.

"Well now, how can we get a donor?"

"For a new born baby, because their organs have a higher chance of regenerating, especially the bone marrow; what you have to do is to sign a few documents, and messages will be sent across to hospitals around the globe with Gloria's picture attached to it. Mind you, no donor will want to give out the bone marrow of his or her child free of charge. So it will cost you a fortune, Daniel."

"Whatever it costs doctor, is nothing compared to my baby's life and I will do anything possible to make her live."

"Alright then, let's hope we get one. We will do our best possible and leave the rest for God. In the meantime, please follow me to my office let us sign the necessary papers."

Daniel stood up, wiped a ball of tears from his eye. He kissed Gloria on her face and left the room with Sonia.

Daniel's parked his car quietly in the garage, he found his way into the sitting room – there he found Nancy lying helplessly on the floor in total darkness.

Nancy's eyes adjusted to the dim light filtering into the living room. It was coming from the door. She perceived Daniel's cologne. She cursed under her breath wishing that she had trusted his intuition. She felt the adrenaline flooding her system - the last thing she wished was for Daniel to start an argument. She wanted to disappear into oblivion.

She breathed deeply, trying to still her heartbeat as Daniel approached her. Memory flooded back as she analyzed the situation in her mind. She sat up as Daniel stood facing her.

"You had no right to deny me of my child's health status you know. I am her father and I have every right to know everything."

"Sonia called you?"

"Yes, she did. Apparently, at least one person knows that I have the right to be aware of what is happening."

"I was… I was going to tell you."

She wanted to stop Daniel from questioning her any further, she wasn't going to tell him, she was going to brood over her misfortune till her breath ceased.

"Maybe you were going to tell me when I'd already lost Gloria. Or maybe you were about telling me from that point you are lying and cowering in your own shadow."

"Please, your words are the last thing I want to hear." she finally let out what she had in mind.

"Why? Will your lying down here bring any solution? Will it bring her health to normal? Or maybe your God will transform everything to normal? Shutting out everyone will not yield any results. We need to face reality as her parents."

She broke down in tears, finally standing up to face Daniel.

"So this is what you came here to do, huh? To torment me? Mock me? Yes! I cannot handle it. I cannot give my daughter life and God cannot heal her, are you satisfied?"

"Is there anything else you need to know? And yes! My God has forsaken me; the God who I lost everything to has forsaken me. He left me at a crossroad and I do not know where to follow. He hates me, I gave you up for him, and I gave my life up for him. He took you away from me and now it is my daughter…. And yes I am in misery." She hurled these words at him in obvious frustration.

"You were so busy preaching to me how loving and caring he is. How miraculous he is. People who believe in those words are the worst lunatic ever. Your God cannot do anything for you! It is just an illusion and it will forever be an illusion of man."

Nancy cried even more.

"The truth hurts, Nancy. At last you have realized that I was right after all; but that is not the issue, the main thing is that Gloria was born with Leukemia and she is at the verge of death, does that sound funny to you? Is this how you were going to take care of her?"

"It hurts me more than what you think, it is taking breath away from..."

"We will find a way out. I have already signed the documents to get another bone marrow for her, I hope we get a donor soon Nancy. Get yourself together. We need to fix this." Daniel interrupted her, not having any patience for self-pity.

He crossed the living room to the kitchen, he made Nancy coffee. "Here," he said, handing her the cup. Nancy grabbed the cup and drank from it.

He watched as Nancy gulped, her eyes swollen from incessant crying. He felt pity for her, but something in the whole situation made him happy- he was right after all, that God did not exist.

Nancy's eyes caught his. Something in him wanted to reach out to her, hug her and assure her that everything will be alright but he felt she had to realize that she was wrong. He wanted her to apologize and acknowledge that he Daniel is the god of her life.

"I will leave now; you should go to the hospital later. Sonia needs you to sign some papers."

Nancy watched him as he left the house. Loneliness struck her. She was angry, angry at herself and angry at the world, even angry at the God she had believed in.

She walked to Gloria's room, whose pictures were strewn everywhere in the room. She grabbed one of the pictures and kissed it.

"I do not know what to do anymore, how could you have cancer baby?" Her voice shook.

"I just want you to be alright. Whatever happened to you should have happened to me instead. You are just a baby Gloria....just a baby."

She hung the picture back; the mirror close to bed caught her attention. She stared back at the haggard face on the mirror - how lean she had become, if only death could suck the rest of life away from her then she would be thanking her stars for relieving her from pressures of the world. But Gloria, who would be with her even in her last minutes before she dies?

"No! She is not going to die!" She screamed, shattering the mirror with a comb from the stand.

She threw herself on the bed, her eyes fixed on the shattered mirror. She fought the world for God but when she needed him, He turned his back on her.

She hurled herself to her feet and walked past the shards of glass on the floor as she heard the doorbell ring. Annabel should better not disturb her with her vain words of encouragement, she thought. She wasn't going to give in to any of those words again.

Hurriedly she tiptoed towards the door, it wasn't Annabel, she opened the door and a postman handed her a piece of documents delivered to her from Royalty hospital. She remembered Daniel had asked her to go to the hospital and sign some documents pertaining to the bone marrow transplant. Nancy signed, thanked the postman and went inside her living room. She grabbed the document she was to read through after staring at it vaguely for minutes.

For two days, Nancy kept reading through the documents and hurling them to the floor. She was lost, she had no idea what she was doing, all she knew was that the world was falling apart and crashing hard on her shoulders. Many times, Sonia and Annabel would call but she kept forwarding their calls, locking herself up in the house and pretending to not be home.

Sonia told Daniel that Nancy was going berserk, no one had heard from her and she hadn't signed the papers. Daniel could do little at the moment because he was out on a crucial business meeting.

Another Sunday morning greeted Nancy and she decided to take a walk around the street and have a feel of what the world looked like now. Had it really fallen? She had no strength, maybe she could just observe the world one more time before probably dying in her sleep. Her mind had been restless – lost between her rosy past and the thorny present.

She stopped by a church and watched as people move in and out of the church auditorium. She gasped at the sight of the crucifix of Jesus on top of the church building. She was startled at a tap on her shoulder; a light-skinned woman was standing beside her.

"Are you going to church ma'am?" The woman asked.

Nancy was numb for a few minutes. She stared at the woman talking to her who somehow, exuded an air of peace around her. The woman smiled at Nancy.

"I am Patricia, would you like to come in?"

Nancy shook her head.

"I wish I could."

"Why not? I will take you into the church and we will welcome…"

"No, I do not want to." She cut her short. "I was just passing by. Your church is beautiful. I will be on my way now, thank you for your concern."

She walked away and the woman said out to her; "You look troubled. He still loves and cares about you, He still loves you. No matter what."

Nancy turned back with tears in her eyes.

"You have no idea. You are wrong ma'am. I am a living disaster and a victim of the wrath of God. I did not do anything, I thought he loved me but no, he doesn't. Please do not tell me about God, there is no God, if there is then He gave up on me long time ago."

"Okay, but please have this flier."

She gave her a piece of paper which contained what looked like religious messages.

"Read it at your own convenience."

Nancy nodded.

"My name is Patricia Maxwell and this is my church, when you are relieved, feel free to come. I am ever willing to listen to you. God is beautiful, life is beautiful."

Nancy looked at her in surprise; she could have said the same of God some days ago. Maybe she hadn't tasted the cruel side of God. Nancy gave her a benign smile and walked away.

She stopped at a mahogany tree and opened the leaflet the lady gave her, perused it and her eyes met lines that captivated her imagination. She read aloud.

"In sickness or ill health; in disappointment or disaster; in loneliness or rejection by even loved ones; in hunger or famine; in hopelessness or despair, God will take care of you. When life seems dark and dreary, and you think you don't have anything to live for anymore, all I know and I am assured of is that God will take care of you. So, if you are contemplating on leaving this great and loving God, just remember this: no one can truly help you in your situation but Him. No sickness defies his attention; no situation escapes him; no problem is too big for him to solve.

As His beloved child, He knows every minute detail of your situation, and He is doing something about it right now. He cares about you; He loves you and He will take care of you."

She could barely read the last words through the tears that brimmed in her eyes...

"Oh God! I am sorry, have mercy on me."

She looked back at the tap on her shoulder to find the same lady Patricia standing close to her again, she was frightened. With tears in her eyes, she asked the lady; "Who are you and why are you following me? You terrify me."

"I am a concerned friend my dear! I have once been distressed like you, may I know your name if you do not mind please?"

"You speak as if you are more than human. I do not understand you."

She looked at her and observed her closely with a deep fear and nervousness. And for a moment, she felt the air of peace hovering around her.

"You are different from anyone I have ever met. You look peaceful. And it is as though something in me is warning me against you. What are you?! Why do you talk to me strangely as though you have known me for ages or what I am going through?"

Patricia smiled.

"I was once close to death and I felt it all over me beckoning my soul and everything in me, I lost the courage to move on because I had no life."

She paused at the sight of a leaf on the ground, looked at it then picked it up.

"I was like this leaf, without a direction because it depends on the wind to blow it away. You might ask what happened to me – I will tell you. The doctor gave me two months to live, I had a terminal illness. I wanted to poison myself because there was no reason to wait that long. One day, a neighbor walked into my house, she told me about a seminar and persuaded me to attend. I said to myself, it is a good way to while away my time while waiting for death. So I went and my faith was lifted, I took down notes then prayed and wept about my life and situation every day for two weeks.

God forgave my sins and healed me of my terminal illness. I lived ma'am, I lived!"

She said this amid tears. "Since then I carry this notebook that I gave to you everywhere I go. It is my miracle. I wrote it and believed in it and it worked for me."

Nancy saw herself smiling heartily. Deep down her heart she longed for a testimony, her own miracle.

Patricia held Nancy's hand.

"Life is like the ocean, it can be still or calm, and rough or rigid but at the end it's always beautiful. You can offer your heart again to God, it is not too late."

"My baby is in the hospital, she has leukemia and I can't do anything." Nancy sobbed.

"I don't want my baby to die, she is at the hospital and I haven't seen her in days – I have had unpleasant experiences ever since I met Jesus. I lost my husband to the world and my baby who was born seven months ago has leukemia. Look at me; I look like a walking corpse. I feel like God abandoned me when I needed him the most."

"We all have our shortcomings and challenges but drifting away from God is like dropping our own life – I do not know how far God can take before He does his things, but all I know is that he will surely do it. Come!" Patricia assured her.

She rose up steering Nancy up as well. "Where are you taking me to? I need to go and see my daughter."

"You will see your daughter but you will need to see God first."

Nancy acquiesced.

CHAPTER TEN

You can't change what was meant to be. Everyone will have that one moment that defines their whole existence... it's fated

Nancy and Patricia walked in to the hospital premises. Sonia was pleased to see her. Sonia gazed at her wild, mussed hair and disheveled dress and wondered what could have been going on with her.

"Nancy dear! I am so pleased to see you at last," Sonia exclaimed, breaking the silence.

"I am sorry doctor, I acted like all hope was lost but I am back here for my daughter," Nancy responded with a mellow voice.

"Yes Nancy, she needs you. Distancing yourself from her will make issues worse for all for us so please take things easy and all will be fine, okay?"

She nodded without much conviction – she introduced Patricia to Sonia as they walked into the ward where Gloria was still lying. Nancy's heart dropped, the tears and fears came back.

"We've not been able to do much for her Nancy. We are still waiting for you. As you know this is a hospital, I have kept Gloria here because I have known you and Daniel for years now and I know what you are going through. But we still have to be professional."

Nancy squeezed her eyes shut and let out a deep breath. She hadn't been a good mother, she knew. She wasn't strong enough to stand for her daughter. She felt sorry for her daughter and sorry for everyone who had tried to tolerate her actions. She needed answers, and Patricia answered her.

"I know what you are thinking, Nancy, you are thinking that cancer is taking your daughter away. Remember God gave you a healthy baby, so you are going to tell him to take the unhealthy one and give you back your Gloria," Patricia told her.

"You will not die Gloria, you will live for mummy and... and your daddy as well, you will live! And I break every yoke of death in your life Gloria, sickness is not your portion because you are the apple of God's eyes. Gloria you are set free from the bondages of leukemia and you are getting out of this sick bed in Jesus name." Nancy's prayer was fervent in its supplication.

"Amen," echoed Sonia and Patricia.

Patricia hugged her.

"Believe and have faith in God and everything will be fine, Nancy."

"I believe! I believe!" she resolved

"That is the spirit my dear, smile for God has conquered death and sickness!"

"Amen! Amen!"

The doctor interjected.

"Daniel has signed for the bone marrow transplant procedure to be carried out and we have issued out notice across the nation for any available bone marrow. Meanwhile she will have to be in this intensive care unit and will keep receiving special attention till we have a donor."

"Gloria will stay at home till we have a donor," Nancy Proclaimed.

Sonia was astonished.

"Do you know what you are saying Nancy? This baby cannot leave till the operation is not carried out. She will die."

"While waiting for a donor, I will wait for a miracle. You can transfer your life support equipment to the house. Whatever it costs, I will pay."

"This is madness!" Sonia exclaimed.

"I don't think I look normal doctor," she replied Sonia politely.

"No doctor, this is faith," Patricia joined

Daniel walked in to the room, and then interrupted them. It was obvious he had been eavesdropping.

"Gloria will stay here. You can't go and sacrifice my daughter on the altar of your barbaric religion. I thought you'd learned your lesson, it's obvious you have not."

All eyes were fixed now on Daniel.

"I am still the controller of the home which I built and you broke, I still have the right to decide what goes on in Gloria's life and you have no right to interfere."

"You are wrong Daniel. The law gave both of us equal right over her. So, you see if I do not consent to this procedure, nothing will happen. It is not only your signature that is needed, mine is needed as well. I don't have strength for this Daniel. Sonia, I would be waiting for the transfer immediately."

She turned to Daniel. "I want to prove you wrong Daniel," she told him as she left the room.

Patricia had to stop on the way to Nancy's house, she encouraged her and reminded her of reasons why she shouldn't give up. Nancy wasn't oblivious of the fact Daniel was following her. She parked her car in the garage and entered her living room.

Daniel's car stopped over and he barged into the house. He met Nancy pacing to and fro.

"What on earth do you think you are doing?"

"The right thing," she answered confidently.

"Are you going insane? What do you think is the right thing? Some days ago you cursed your God and today you are head over heels in love with him again that you are so confident he will heal my baby? You need a psychiatrist, Nancy."

"I am sound and alright. You mocked me because you think that my God is not capable of healing Gloria but I stand to tell you this day that He will."

"I will not argue with you so much on this but I will make you a promise woman! If I lose my baby, I will take your breath away."

"Even if you are not happy with yourself Nancy, don't drag Gloria into this."

Nancy looked at him; she could sense his fear even in his threats. She smiled at his rising anger as a peaceful calm descended on her.

Daniel blindly walked away, banging the door behind him.

"It is your battle Lord, not mine, it is your battle!"

That evening, Daniel stomped into Edward's living room, where he met Edward and his Wife,

Christie on the sofa. Daniel, not knowing what to say sat down wearily on the sofa. Edward walked across to him.

"All my life, all these time that I have known you Daniel, I have never seen you this way. I am here man; tell me who did this to you?"

He gave Edward a sober gaze and sat up. "I shouldn't have been born on this planet."

"Edward, Christie, Gloria has cancer. Leukemia."

Christy who had been engrossed in a television program lost her grip on the remote and it clattered to the tiled floor.

"You must be kidding me, how come Daniel?" She asked.

"Daniel, is this some sort of joke or something?" Edward joined.

"I want to know where I had it wrong"

Daniel glanced around Edward's house, his eyes turned red - sadness brimming in his irises. He quickly wiped his eyes. He was about to cry, Edward and Christy felt pity for him.

"As I speak to you right now, she is lying like a rock in the hospital."

"Is this nemesis or what? But I've been good to people. I've been good to you." He finally let the tears roll.

Edward hugged his friend, "The reality of the world is that, it is cruel. Really cruel."

Daniel paid no attention; he dragged his dazed self out of the room, ignoring Edward and Christy as they called out to him.

"I pity Daniel," Edward stated the obvious.

"It is their problem, let them handle it" Christy said abruptly.

Daniel's car stopped over at a church. The lights were on but he could find no one inside. He walked into it, not knowing what he was doing. He smirked; this was going to be harder than he thought.

"I do not know why many people believe in you so much. I have never felt you around me or your miracles but they say you are miracle working God. What do you think of me? Am I vile? Am I full of dirty thoughts? But of what value is it to be virtuous? What pleasure comes from serving you? What gratification can come from self-denial? As far as I am concerned there is no God that cares, a few years from now, we all die and we will be forgotten even by our loved ones. You turned my wife against me. You make her murder me with cruel words and I am now worthless before her." He spewed those words as he climbed the altar.

"But see here, I cannot pray because I do not know how to... people trust you. But how can one trust you when one can barely trust one's self?" He laughed scornfully.

"See, I do not know what I am doing but I just feel like talking to something that cannot reply me. Something that will keep shut and just listen, something like you."

He stood up.

"I am about leaving – in case you can speak please do not tell my ex-wife Nancy, your lover, the one you snatched from me that I was here. Do not ever tell her that."

He fidgeted as he was leaving, as response to a feeling that he couldn't fathom. He hurriedly left the church, entering his car and racing away.

Daniel finally settled in a cozy hotel room, he couldn't go back to his penthouse. Should he die in his sleep, he will be found much earlier, he thought.

He reminisced on how he planned his life with Nancy and how things were turning out to be – for years, he'd thought his plans were working out fine until Nancy's conversion. He'd ask for a way to make things better but he could not fathom a way to force Nancy to do his bidding. As he lay on the bed, he felt disturbed in his heart that he had done something bad for him to be suffering like this. "But I didn't do anything na," He tried to convince himself.

"Is Nancy feeling the same way I am feeling, Miserable and disgusted? What is it that is making her feel so comfortable in this adversity?" He questioned himself.

Daniel was lying on the bed motionless when his phone rang, it was his secretary. For a minute he hesitated before taking the call, but realized only an emergency would make his assistant call him now.

He sprang up from the bed on realizing that it was a matter of high urgency. He checked his time and to his utter amazement, he had slept through half of the day. He quickly dressed up and rushed out, not minding his appearance.

He entered his office, ignoring the numerous eyes that were fixed on him. He met the startled face of Silas, Global Tech manager.

"I will explain," He blurted to Silas.

"That was not supposed to be a greeting, Daniel, is it...?" Silas smirked.

"Forgive my manners Silas. Please do not do this to me...I owe Glotech a good apology and I am willing to explain everything sir please."

Daniel was apologizing; he had a contract to execute for Glotech which had been lying on his table for months.

"I am not the right person to apologize to. Our CEO is on his way to Germany for a tour so please, I am nobody here - And it is his order that the contract papers be retrieved from you." Silas calmly told him.

"I know there is something you can do for me on this and I am willing to pay you any amount to make sure that I do not lose the contract. I am begging you."

"I can do nothing. You showed your incompetence and left a contract of two weeks for more than month without doing a single thing about it. Please Daniel, you know too well that begging will not solve this... this is work." He stated.

"Silas, I have been through hell these past few weeks. My daughter was dying...my wife has been tormenting me..." He stopped on noticing the smile on Silas' face.

"You let your family issues put you away from your work man. I pity you. Your family will always be there but once you lose a job, you have lost it. We all have issues, but we don't let it get to us."

"Miracles do happen my friend, the shortest distance between a problem and a solution is the distance between your knee and the floor. Pray to God! If there is something He can do for you, he will do."

He grabbed the files that brought him down to Daniel and rose to leave. "And it might interest you to know that it is your friend's company that won the contract – Edward Sterling and they are already at work."

Daniel felt breath been taken away from him as he heard the name; 'Edward sterling'

He was dumbfounded. Silas walked away from the office leaving Daniel to himself.

A smile that was half sweet and half cruel took over his lips. The bitter truth was so resounding that the echo got his being numb. He wanted to shout, he wanted to cry. But altogether, he did both, causing the staff company to run into his office. He yelled at them to leave him alone.

Edward? His best friend? He was perplexed. What was happening to the world? Everything he thought was true was in fact a lie.

"Oh goodness! What is happening to me?" He wondered.

Memories of how his company won the contract rose in his mind - he'd gone out with Edward for a brief meeting when they ran into Silas. He told them that their company has been trying his contact but couldn't reach him. They exchanged contact and scheduled the day for a proper meeting.

Few days after their meeting, Glotech was pleased with his proposal and the contract was awarded to him, little did he know that Edward had been spying on him, to take advantage of his slip.

"Friends were meant to stand for each other goddammit!" He said with every ounce of fury in him.

"How could Edward do this to me?" He wailed.

He had tried to rack his brains as to where he went wrong. How he did not see the signs? They still went out often, even during stormy months with Nancy. They'd talked every now and then, and he even encouraged him when he was downtrodden.

"He was family for crying out loud." He growled.

Family?

There was obviously none now; everyone he trusted had now left him. He was a lone man, he thought. Maybe karma was beating him at his own game. He'd extorted money from associates and even dragged them for accusing him. However, they were foolish, he reminded himself.

He rose to his feet and staggered blindly out to the street. It was raining quite heavily but he had no intentions of driving himself so he walked under the rain. He was so soaked; he didn't know whether he was actually crying because the droplets of rain on his might have mixed up with his tears.

Daniel, for once, in all the years of his life, felt that this god of rain was possibly washing away the sins of the world. He yelled; passersby looked at him - a strange mad man. He walked in the middle of the road wishing for a car to hit him but vehicles were avoiding him.

CHAPTER ELEVEN

*** I was in the darkness for long, I almost became darkness***

When Daniel got back to his house, he was lost between the thought of confronting Edward and the thought of ending his miserable life. He rose and staggered blindly to his bar – he grabbed a bottle of whiskey and gulped from the bottle. As he drank, his eyes were filled with tears which streamed down like never before. Broken, he smashed the empty bottle of whiskey to the floor. He remembered how life had been for him, how he had meandered through it, how life has twisted him, how hard it was to live now.

Drowsy, he rose and made for the kitchen – close to the kitchen door, he missed his step, fell to the floor and promptly lost consciousness.

That Saturday, Nancy walked up to the doctor. She was ready for her baby to be transferred to her home. Annabel, Patricia and Pastor Gabriel were all there to help her out.

"I hope you know what you are doing and when you come to the realization that you are going the wrong way, it will not be too late for you? Besides, where is Daniel? He ought to be here with you and be aware that your baby is no longer in my custody for now."

Nancy smiled. Daniel didn't have to be there. He was just Gloria's father; he wasn't there when she was in pains, he wasn't there when her water broke and he wasn't there when Gloria was christened. The only he privilege he had was the fact that the law made him a father. But through it all she still respected him. She still wore her ring on her finger.

"I am grateful for what you have done so far and for your understanding too. Thank you, I have not heard from Daniel and he has not called."

"I hope all is well with him; the last time he came here, he seemed devastated."

Nancy nodded. She hoped that all was well with Daniel too.

One of the nurses preparing Gloria for the transfer walked into the consulting room and informed them that everything was ready.

Sonia looked at Nancy; she took her hand in hers.

"I do not know much about God; I have heard testimonies though but may your faith save you. Thank you for signing these documents. We will begin our search immediately. Do not hesitate to call me if anything comes up."

"You have amazing friends by the way" Sonia told Nancy, referring to Annabel, Patricia and Pastor Gabriel who had been her rock. Even during moments when she faltered, they stood in the gap for her; visiting Gloria and praying for her. Indeed, they are amazing, Nancy agreed.

"They are awesome. Thank you, Sonia, thanks Pat, Anna and Pastor Gabriel. I am immensely indebted to all of you. This path that I trod is not easy, but with you guys I can conquer the world."

They all chuckled.

"Please, go now." Sonia said, after they hugged.

The hospital van stopped in Nancy's compound and Glory was brought inside, she was laid on the bed and the nurse started dressing her up. She had been on drip for days and her breath was gradually leaving her. Nancy looked at the nurse as she observed Gloria's pulse.

"She has just days to go Nancy." The nurse said, sympathetically.

"No! She has years to live. I will see her children walk in this compound, nurse! Gloria will be a living miracle," She replied the nurse, making her smile slightly. The door opened and Patricia and the others walked into the room.

"We would like to pray for her." Patricia said.

"I will be on my way now, but please always give her some space." The nurse told Nancy before leaving.

Nancy knew this was not going to be easy but she was determined now more than ever to see the greatness of God. It might tarry a while but she was sure he would surely do it.

Patricia held hands with the rest and she led the prayers for Gloria.

As Daniel lay unconsciously on the ground, he fell into a trance in his unconscious state. It was his own day of retribution and fate hit him so hard. It was at this juncture that he knew that the devil had been his master.

There was thunder and wild tumult – the harsh glare of lightning, the shattering roar of great waves leaping mountains high and hissing asunder in mid-air. Elements let loose in a boisterous dance of death. In the trance, Daniel staggered at his feet but was pulled back to the ground with a force that was mightier than his own.

He heard voices. Thunder rolled across the sky and lightning crashed. Fire lit up the heavens above him and flashed down to earth as if to strike him.

"Woe to the world and to men of the world." The voice said.

The otherworldly sound in these words filled him with such horror that he fell on his knees in intense misery and almost prayed to the God he had through all his life disbelieved in and denied. But he was too mad with fear to find words - the dense darkness - the horrid uproar of the wind and sea – the infuriated and confused shouting...

Suddenly, a swirling sound from the wind slammed his face hard and his head snapped sideways. The stinging blow made his head reel and spin - fierce cries mingled with the jarring thunder.

"Come with me, Daniel Frank."

The voice beckoned Daniel, and as he spoke to him, all self-possession deserted Daniel and he stretched out his hands to a force that made itself visible now as a big and wild human. Appealingly, he gave his hands not knowing what he was doing.

"Oh God!" Daniel cried.

He was silenced by a great power.

"Spare me your prayers, for God's sake, for your own sake and for mine! Follow!"

Panic struck Daniel as he heard the voice saying aloud:

"Away! All ye devils of the sea, air and earth. Ye who are not God's elements but my servants. The unrepentant souls of men! Lost in the graves, waves, whichever ye made your destiny! Away! Stop your clamor! This hour is Mine!"

The faceless force faced Daniel. "Do you know me, Or do you need me to tell you who I am?"

Daniel's lips moved but he could not speak, the dreadful truth that was dawning was yet too frenzied to be uttered by a mortal like him.

"Be dumb! Be motionless! But hear and feel – by the supreme power of God – for there is no power in heaven or on earth."

"You are chosen, Daniel, son of Frank. You are chosen to learn your lessons that all men still doubt.

You are one of the world's fortunate men – you can buy this world's goodness with your ill-gotten money but in this realm you are stripped naked – we behold you as a shameless egoist, persistently engaged in defacing their divine image of immortality – and for that sin there is no excuse and no escape but punishment. How dare you say there is no God?! Whosoever prefers self to God and in the arrogance of that self; presumes doubt and denies, God invites another power to encompass his destiny. The power of evil! Made evil and kept evil by the disobedience of man alone - that power whom mortals call Satan, the prince of darkness.

Do you know me now?"

Daniel sat, rigid.

"You, by the mercy of the creator's will, are permitted to see everything in the universe. But yet you are blind to things divine even when your wife brought light to your home, you were still blind! And because you cannot see, you doubt! Arrogant fool! Men reject light and accept me and I enter and give them all they want... everything!"

Daniel shuddered involuntarily as he began to realize the awful nature he had been allowing to fester within him.

"I have chosen you because you are an apparently respected man – you manage to conceal your criminal records– you have murdered no one- your lack of chastity and adulteries are those of every fashionable vice - monger and your blasphemies against God are no worse than those of the most approved modern magazine contributors but you are nevertheless guilty of the sin – sensual egotism. The murderer may repent and atone for the souls he has laid waste, the adulterer may scourge himself and do heartfelt penance and the blasphemer may be forgiven of blasphemy. But to the egotist there is no chance of wholesome penitence, since to himself he is perfect, and he counts himself as someone superior.

But when God is forgotten and love is mocked then the end is near. I take my part in this END for the soul of man is not done with when the leave their fleshly tenements."

The uproar of thunder and the clashing of the wind arose again and Daniel found himself wailing and in agony... he thought it was too late for him.

"Oh no! I must be dreaming," Daniel said to himself.

"Man! Deceive not thy self for thou are awake – not sleeping, you are flesh as well as spirit. This place is neither hell nor heaven nor the world to which thou know but this is just a passing phase to eternity in as much as God surrounds all universe! Fate strikes this hour – and in this hour is given thee to choose thy master.

But take heed lest thou forget that among men I am a man! In human form I move with all humanity through endless ages – to kings and counselors, to priests and scientists, to thinkers and teachers, to old and young, I come in the shape of their pride or vices and I am as one with all. The selfish finds in me another ego – but for the pure in heart, the high in faith, the perfect in intention, I do retreat with joy.

Therefore, Daniel the vile son of Frank... you are lucky amongst men to be given a second chance by the God of all creation. If by my will, you will be rotting in hell; where many of whom you know willfully made their abode; they heard the word of God but did not believe in Him. Choose and change not in any time hereafter whom thou – this hour, this time in thy last probation – choose I say! Will thou serve self and me or God only?"

Daniel looked from right to left, the question seemed like a thunder to his ears. He saw a gathering crowd of faces, all white, wistful, wondering, threatening and imploring. They were pressing him with glistening eyes and lips that moved silently. And as they were staring at him, he saw a spectral thing – the image of himself- he was poor and frail, ignorant and undiscerning – limited in both capacity and intelligence, yet full of strange egotism. He saw the image of his sick baby with one of the white clad creature. At the other side he saw Nancy, sitting majestically on a throne – another white creature standing close to her holding a crown with it. He recognized with shame his puny attempts at scorning God and his worthless effrontery and blasphemies against Him. And in a sudden repudiation of his own worthless existence, he found both voice and speech, Daniel echoed aloud;

"God! God only…" He cried.

"Annihilation at his hands, rather than life without Him. God only, I have chosen! Have mercy on me!"

The sky blazed firmly into fiery gold and Daniel was seized by compelling hands and held firmly down.

He still murmured.

God! God only! No other except him… it's you God, only you…

Nancy was sitting on the couch lost in deep thought, her countenance was perturbed yet inside her she felt a surge of hope rising. Every now and then Nancy would walk to and fro in the living room with nothing in mind. She was on the verge of lifting her bible when she heard a cry in the bedroom.

Nancy sat down – paying attention to what she erroneously thought was going on in her mind.

"Have I started hearing Gloria's voice even in my mind? Oh God, help me." she heaved.

The crying became louder and more persistent – Nancy almost tore her cotton gown as she ran upstairs. As she opened the door to her bedroom, she saw Gloria on the bed crying, the life supporting devices that was fixed on her were no longer in their position. Agitated, Nancy, for a minute, got numb – she rushed to her baby and jerked her up. With tears streaming down her cheeks, she exclaimed. Her shock at the situation quickly gave way for Gloria to gain pleasure at the state she met her baby in. "Oh God! This is You!"

She rested Gloria at the crook of her left arm and couldn't help but sing aloud with a teary voice. The baby's cries ceased, Nancy examined her child and noticed that Gloria was perfectly okay. She expressed her joy with the lifting of her hands on high.

Nancy rushed downstairs with Gloria still on her arms. She picked her phone and dialed the Sonia's number.

The doctor was in her office with a nurse, giving her instruction on what to do when her phone rang

"Please come to my house immediately, Gloria is awake and she has been crying...please come as quick as possible." She told Sonia, fidgeting.

"This cannot be!" Sonia said as she exchanged glances with the standing nurse, whose faced showed curiousity.

"The baby is alive, I will have to go and confirm. Take care of the hospital for me."

She picked up her bag, removed her lab coat and left the hospital.

Daniel got up from the position he was lying. Empty bottles of alcohol scattered around him. He wept uncontrollably. He stood up, he felt how dirty he was, everything around him was a mess but inside him, a peace he never knew surrounded him. Hours ago he was bound but now, he was liberated. He was fully conscious of his freedom and peace - his next thought was his family - his beloved wife and sick baby. They were pure. Unbeknown to him, God had already visited his home.

"Thank You Lord for this." he managed to voice out.

Sonia barged into the house and saw Nancy carrying Gloria.

"Doctor!" Nancy called out.

She gave Gloria to her without hesitation. The doctor held her, examined her body but couldn't find the symptoms of leukemia that were previously all over her. She did the examination countless times but found nothing. Happily, she screamed;

"This is a miracle! I have never seen but heard! Nancy, this is a miracle!"

"Your God is great!" she cried out in joy.

"No Doctor, our God is great." She corrected her.

"I have done a lot of things against him, I am not sure he will look upon me with mercy." Sonia cried.

"There is no sin that is not pardonable before God if you confess with a pure heart. He is always there to forgive and forget. My dear doctor, pray to him sincerely and you will see him working wonders in your life." Nancy said those words of assurance with so much conviction.

The door quietly opened and Daniel walked in gently, they fixed their eyes on him and before Nancy could utter a word, he said;

"Darling, I have met Him too," he proclaimed amid tears.

With hope surging in her, she asked, "You have met who?"

"I have found Christ!" He blurted.

The air was filled with shouts of liberation; Daniel knelt down before Nancy sobbing.

"Forgive me my love, for my wasted years, for all I have put you through in the past. The devil had my soul but God showed me mercy."

Nancy put her hands in his and pulled him up, a smile playing on her lips and tears flowing down her cheeks. Daniel stood.

"You can only kneel before our God my dear husband." She said, nodding her head simultaneously.

"Yes! You are my husband; you didn't cease to be, even for a day, my Daniel. I was just waiting on God to touch you, but all these while, I've always been there."

Daniel wiped her tears away; they both looked at the doctor carrying their baby. Nancy broke the good news to him.

"It is all over now." She said smiling. "Our baby has been made whole. Gloria is perfectly okay!"

"Oh blessed Jesus!" Daniel exclaimed, walking towards his daughter.

"The doctor certified as well. God has done it."

Tears of joy streamed down her cheeks again.

Daniel carried her in his arms, walked toward Nancy and gathered her in his arms too, they looked at the doctor and the trio smiled all over.

"I should have met this God earlier," Daniel said, to Nancy's laughter.

"Come on Daniel, we have a lot of work to do on you. I need to dial Annabel and pastor Gabriel!"

IFEOMA IRENE UGBOMA is a Nigerian writer, girl-child advocate, educator and peace advocate. She is also a certified safety officer, oil and gas document controller and a first aid administrator.

Motivated by her strong passion for creating solutions, Ifeoma has done extensive research on ways to address the common factors responsible for the social, physical, mental and spiritual development of humans, with a special focus on the girl-child. This is what inspired her to find KISMET FOUNDATION, an organization established for the purpose of empowering young girls and revitalizing the value of education. She also volunteers as the Nigerian Ambassador for Peace Aid International and Ileral Nigeria.

Ifeoma presently studies Radiography and Environmental Science, and Resource Management at the University of Uyo, Akwa-Ibom state, Nigeria and the National Open University of Nigeria (NOUN) respectively. ECHOES OF MERCY is her first book.